The dark sea closed around them

Geoff Bishop lay back in the water, holding Nanos across the chest with one arm and sculling gently with the other. The yacht seemed to have given up the search. The spotlight still trailed along the water, but at some distance from the smoldering debris that remained afloat. The lights along the shores of the bay twinkled in the distance.

Alone, Bishop knew he could make it. But he didn't know if he had the strength to keep Nanos afloat. The immediate problem was Alex's wound. Somehow he had to stop the bleeding.

Blood.

A warning bell sounded in the back of Bishop's mind.

Blood attracks sharks.

And then Geoff Bishop looked up and saw them, barely thirty feet away, lit from behind by the light of the yacht.

The dagger tips of two dorsal fins cut slowly through the waves of Tampa Bay.

SOBs
SOLDIERS OF BARRABAS

SOBs
SOLDIERS OF BARRABAS

FIRESTORM U.S.A.

JACK HILD

A GOLD EAGLE BOOK FROM
WORLDWIDE

TORONTO • NEW YORK • LONDON • PARIS
AMSTERDAM • STOCKHOLM • HAMBURG
ATHENS • MILAN • TOKYO • SYDNEY

First edition January 1987

ISBN 0-373-61616-3

Special thanks and acknowledgment to
Robin Hardy for his contributions to this work.

Printed in Canada

1

Needle-sharp splinters lanced across Nile Barrabas's face as bullets pounded into the door of the white stucco villa. The black-garbed mercenary dived forward, twisting his body around to aim for the fading muzzle-flash high in the darkened house.

He squeezed the liquid trigger of his MAC-10, and blue-tailed comets leaped from the barrel. As he slammed into the floor near a staircase, a scream split the darkness. Moments letter the terrorist's body thudded to the floor beside him.

There was another shout of panic and a rifle crashed to the floor, both sounds undercut by the ceaseless chatter of autofire. Barrabas rolled into a crouch, turning to see Lee Hatton fire from the door. A shadow darted through the deep gray light and disappeared. The woman warrior slid quickly into the house.

They were frozen in a moment of silence.

Barrabas signaled to her with a nod. They moved in, their ears straining, the silent human radar scanning into the blank unknown ahead. There were men in the dark, empty lakeside villa, armed men who had been programmed to kill. They had no choices to make. They were the lucky ones. Barrabas needed prisoners, like it or not, to answer a few questions. But he hadn't left Vietnam alive without learning that, in battle, there was only one choice to be made—victory or death. He had made his choice a few moments earlier in the split second he raised his foot and kicked in the front door. He was going to win. The target was a terrorist suicide squad preparing to strike an unknown target in central Florida. It wasn't going to be easy.

Barrabas and Hatton heard a faint tapping through the doorway to a large sunroom. A distant bluish light wavered faintly against the walls. The two mercs reacted, stealthily moving away from either side of the doorframe, crouching and raising their submachine guns. A shriek ripped the darkness, followed by the sound of running boots. The doorway exploded with spurts of muzzle fire as one of the terrorists raced into the hallway in a suicidal, all-or-nothing frenzy. His bullets cut through the air toward Lee Hatton.

Barrabas squeezed again, peppering the darkness and the fanatic with 9 mm death studs at 1,100 rounds a minute. Not fast enough. Lee flew back, dropping to the floor.

"Dear God, no." Barrabas gritted his teeth as the white heat of rage coursed through him. His autofire struck home, punching through the terrorist's body and holding it upright for an instant in a wild jerky dance. The dead man dropped, twitching as life made its final exit. Barrabas rushed past, continuing the arc of autofire in the next room. A wall of glass facing onto a swimming pool shattered, and crystal waves pounded on the linoleum beach. A third terrorist burst from behind swaths of crashing drapery. Autodeath winged past Barrabas's cheek and shoulder. He pivoted toward the attacker and ripped the barrel upward.

The MAC-10's firepower flung the terrorist backward, halfway through the broken window. The attacker's scream cut out as a three-foot spike of pointed plate glass impaled him back to front, severing his spinal cord. The bloody tip rose slowly through his guts, and his body sank. The man's hands fell back, and he hung motionlessly, his eyes open and glazed by death.

Pool lights beneath the surface of the aqua-blue water shone into the house, casting shadowy ripples against Barrabas's thin blackened face. The cold bluish light deepened the determined line of his gaunt scarred cheeks and tight lips. The lone merc crouched and listened.

On the far side of the terrace, a tube of purple light in a wire cage hummed and sizzled playfully, instantaneously electrocuting adoring insects. Carefully and quickly Barrabas retreated to the room where Lee Hatton had fallen. The slender muscular woman pushed herself from the floor and rose to her feet, her face white. She swung her MAC-10 up and paced back against a wall, glancing quickly at the colonel. He read her eyes. Even with a bullet-proof vest, she had taken the terrorist's fire like a wallop from a weighted boxing glove.

Wordlessly they moved back into the sunroom, avoiding the shards of glass glittering on the tile. The remains of the shattered wall separated the two mercs from the pool and terrace like a fence of sharp jagged teeth. The impaled terrorist's blood streamed down the broken window and formed puddles on the floor.

The mercs strained to hear over the chirping symphony of crickets in the night outside. The dead man's body swayed slightly. The fragmented sections of plate glass remaining in the broken wall creaked.

A doorway on the far side of the room led into another wing of the house. Barrabas swung his MAC quickly toward the dark opening. He darted across it and ducked into a corner beside the shattered wall. The terrace around the pool was surrounded by a low tile wall and leafy bushes that had been laboriously manicured into perfect spheres. The height of the palm trees beyond the pool area indicated a drop of six to eight feet to the lawns that ran down to the lake. There was no breeze. Hatton stood in the doorway that led back to the hall, frozen in concentration. Working feverishly, Barrabas ripped the nearly empty mag from his MAC-10 and replaced it with a fresh one.

Suddenly a low wail rose from somewhere in the gardens behind the villa, modulating sharply to the eerie yodel of a baying coyote, the call of the predator, the howl of the meat eater. The leaves in a row of manicured bushes on the far side of the pool stirred and twitched.

Barrabas waited, aiming his submachine gun slightly ahead of the moving shrubbery. It was a matter of a few stretched seconds that seemed like hours.

The animal call rose feverishly again from the grounds of the estate, chilling the night.

A man jumped from behind the bush, confusion on his face clear in the bluish light cast from the pool. Hatton ran forward firing. The fugitive jumped onto the wall and swung his automatic rifle toward the house. He loosed a rapid river of autofire as a second man made a run from the bushes.

What was left of the windows exploded. Deadly slivers of glass flew into the house. Hatton dived into a corner for cover. The man on the wall froze as tiny circles across his chest suddenly blew outward. Gore spewed across the terrace, flecking the cool blue waters of the pool with undulating red clouds. The terrorist fell backward, disappearing behind the wall. Somewhere in the gardens, Billy Two, the third merc in the attack force, had made his aim good.

Now Barrabas let it rip, firing low at the last terrorist, who was fleeing along the edge of the pool. The fugitive screamed as bullets blasted across his arm and shoulder. His automatic rifle flew into the pool and sank. The force of the bullets spun him around. He fell, sliding along the terrace until he came to a halt near the electric mosquito zapper. Barrabas eased off the trigger. The villa and its gardens were quiet. Once again the night was given over to the chirrupping of contented crickets. Nature, as always, was oblivious to the carnage. Death, having visited for a few moments, slipped quietly away.

The mercenary leader strode onto the terrace, stepping over the upright glass shards. He kept his gun trained on the one living terrorist. The man stood and coldly surveyed his captors. His Asian face was drained of color, and soft rapid breaths escaped his lips. His eyes were calculating, showing no sign of pain from the wound on his arm. Barrabas had seen it before. Fanaticism was its own anesthetic.

"Looks like we got one of them alive, Dr. Hatton," Barrabas said, turning to the woman fighter as she stepped through the wall of broken glass. "You better look him over and stop the bleeding so he can talk."

Billy Starfoot, nicknamed Billy Two by Barrabas's team of mercenary warriors, ran up the stone steps at one side of the terrace. Like Barrabas and Lee Hatton, he wore black fatigue pants, but the full-blooded Osage was barefoot and shirtless. His black face paint extended over his massive shoulders, arms and chest, and was dabbed with streaks of red and white. The Indian claimed the warpaint protected him in battle. He carried a MAC-10 in his right hand, and a belt of spare mags hung around his waist.

"Good shooting," Barrabas said. "And a great imitation of a coyote."

"Coyote was not me. Was coyote spirit I called to help us."

"Whatever you say, Billy."

Lee Hatton, who supplemented her talents in the martial arts with a medical degree, moved cautiously around the pool toward the wounded man. The terrorist continued to stare at them, one arm raised, the other hanging uselessly at his side. His eyes darted around the terrace, seeking an avenue of escape.

"Don't bother," Barrabas told him. "You're not going anywhere. Not until we get the information we want."

The man turned his head toward the merc leader and curled his lip. Still showing no signs of pain, he raised his head haughtily.

"We have come upon your land as a swarm of flies upon a rotting carcass, American. Like flies we will multiply. Do you think by swatting one of us or two or a hundred you will do anything to eliminate us? Since we heard of your arrival, many others were evacuated from here in time, leaving only a few of us to kill as many of you as we could. We are gladly martyrs. For every one of us dead, ten more will rise up to defeat you, stupid American!"

The terrorist spat out the last word like an oath. He hooked his foot around one of the legs supporting the metal cage of the mosquito zapper and dove toward the pool. Billy Two leaped forward, preparing to dive as terrorist and zapper plunged into the water, the electrical cord trailing behind. Barrabas grabbed the Indian and jerked him back. A flash of light sparked on the surface of the pool as the purple light and electrified coils of the zapper went in after the terrorist. Water splashed onto the terrace from the impact. As the electric current sped through the highly conductive water molecules, the Asian trembled and stiffened, his eyes bulging from their sockets. His skin turned a deep purplish blue. He sank several feet under the surface before rising slowly to the top, where he floated, dead.

"Our friends, the federal agents, will be here any minute now," Lee reminded them. "After the weight we pulled to get in here first, they're not going to be too happy about all the bodies lying around."

Barrabas nodded toward the dead man floating in the pool. "He told us one important thing before being poached. Someone told them we were coming. They were tipped off in time to get out before we arrived. It's what I suspected. An operation like this needs help inside the United States."

"That means they've got people working for them somewhere," said Billy Two.

"Yup. Somewhere inside the same information line we're using."

"The only information sources we have are a couple of secret government agencies," Lee pointed out. "That leads us to a pretty chilling conclusion."

"A traitor," Billy Two boomed darkly. "And we are on the firing line."

"Let's fan out and look around the house before the government boys get here," Barrabas ordered. "Lee and Billy Two, check the bodies."

He stepped back through the wall of broken glass and walked through the house, flicking on lights. Bare bulbs in overhead fixtures harshly illuminated the empty rooms of the fashionable Winter Park villa. The floors were scattered with ground-out cigarette butts and torn packages of junk food. In one room, several sleeping bags and some crates of ammunition lay in a heap against a wall. He leaned down to pick up a small piece of yellow paper that caught his eye. It was a numbered receipt of some kind. He slipped it into his pocket.

"Colonel," Lee Hatton called to him, approaching from the hallway. "The bodies are clean. Not a single piece of ID, but I think we'll find some of the faces in the rogues' gallery of international terrorists. Two were Asians, probably Japanese Red Guard. One I recognized as Italian Red Brigade. Two more look Middle Eastern, and considering his blond hair I'd say the one who fell from the stairs was German, Red Army maybe. And these are all over." She held out a palmful of cigarette butts and a crumpled package.

"Juno," Barrabas said, reading the brand name printed in tiny gold letters under the short white filters and on the package.

Hatton nodded. "West German cigarettes. The rest are all bad old-fashioned Marlboros."

The sound of racing car engines and screaming tires reverberated from the front of the villa. Through the open doors, the mercs saw a half dozen giant black Oldsmobiles drive up and park in front of the house. A pair of federal agents in expensive designer suits emerged from each car. They swarmed into the villa, their gold Rolexes glinting in the bright lights. The pastel police had arrived. It was time to get out.

"Colonel Barrabas!"

A tall young man with a white sports jacket and two days' growth of fuzz on his chin sauntered toward him.

"No prisoners," the man said matter-of-factly. "You promised us prisoners, Colonel, and we're shit out of luck. How do you suppose we're to going find out what in hell's going on if there's no one to question? Or is it against your principles to leave them alive?"

Barrabas grimaced coldly. Johnny Burton was a big-city shooter, the coordinator of the special antiterrorist effort ordered by the attorney general to deal with the present crisis. He was hung up on style and was the kind of keener whose scruples were often fewer than those of the criminals and terrorists he built his career on.

"Someone tipped them off, Burton."

"Don't give me that. Just remember, I'm the one that has to go before the cameras on the six o'clock news. I'm the one who has to explain how a bunch of people got shot up and why the police weren't there until it was all over. I'm concerned, Barrabas, because I know you're not coming clean with me. You're operating behind my back."

"I'm not accountable to you, Burton. And my men aren't, either."

"You've got only two of your men here. What are the other four up to? I want to know."

It was the one ace Barrabas still had up his sleeve, and he wasn't going to play it with Johnny Burton. A powerful spotlight descended from heaven and circled the grounds outside the villa. It was followed by the loud chopping of a helicopter landing. Barrabas ignored Burton and walked outside onto the steps.

The Miami hotshot pushed up the sleeves of his white jacket and grabbed Barrabas's arm as he went by. Barrabas stopped, barely constraining the urge to slam his fist into the agent's fuzzy face. The thought of the innocent lives at stake stopped him. He grabbed Burton's hand just behind the knuckles. There were four thin bones branching into fingers. Barrabas squeezed tightly, grinding them together. The muscles in Burton's face tightened. He jerked his hand away.

"This is going to count against you next time we get a lead, Barrabas," he said with unconcealed hostility. "I've got friends in high places, you know. Influential friends."

"Is that what matters to you, Burton? Being a front-page hero?" Barrabas jabbed a long hard finger into the detective's chest. "Burton, we've got a serious problem on our hands. And I don't care who gets a gold star for the cleanup. I already know it won't be me or any of my men, because that's the way we operate. We'll stop these bloodsuckers, Burton, with your help or without it.''

The state agent backed off, waving his arms and trying to smile his way through the scene. ''Whatever you say, Colonel. Just remember this. I'm legit and so are my boys. If anyone finds out you're working on this, your ass fries.'' Burton smiled a long row of white pearlies. ''If I were you, I'd watch what kind of profile I kept. Or I'll plaster your face under the Wanted sign in every post office in the country.''

Lee Hatton appeared at Barrabas's side. ''Colonel, chopper's waiting.''

Barrabas turned back to Burton one more time. ''Remember this, Burton. I've got one face and one heart. There's someone out there with two faces and no heart at all.

''Burton's smile vanished. He shifted to his other foot and regarded the mercenary with worried skepticism.

''What do you mean?'' he sneered. Barrabas walked.

There was a traitor and a pack of mad-dog terrorists on the loose in America's vacation state. It was as sure as sunshine that if they weren't stopped, the Caribbean Sea would turn crimson with Florida's blood.

''Whaddya mean, Barrabas? Hey! Whaddya mean!'' Burton's derisive shouts followed the mercenary leader across the lawn as he ran toward the waiting helicopter.

2

The National Guard helicopter followed the southwest coast of Florida. Outside the windows, the night blanketed their progress. For an hour, Nile Barrabas had followed the lights of the cities, islands of civilization strung along the beaches of the Gulf of Mexico: Sarasota, Punta Gorda, Fort Myers, Cape Coral, Naples. Abruptly the land fell into darkness as the vast Everglades took over, sprawling far into the interior.

He turned from the window and settled deeper into his seat. The dull steady grind of the Bell 214C's Lycoming engines seemed louder now that the view outside the window was no longer diverting. Across from him, a man with dark blond hair and green eyes wore a U.S. Army officer's uniform. The soldier had introduced himself simply as Major Landry Carter when they picked him up at MacDill. Neither of them had said a word since then. Now, with Carter staring forlornly into space, Barrabas let his mind wander back to the events of the previous seven days.

A week earlier six submersible swimmer-delivery vehicles were found abandoned on beaches up and down the Florida coast. Each one had the capability of secretly landing six men on American soil. A few days later a shipment of arms destined for military bases in Panama City was hijacked on an interstate highway. Later, a routine drug raid on a Miami mansion unexpectedly netted some of the stolen explosive devices. And when the shooting was over, the bodies of six known terrorists, fugitives from international justice, were identified in the debris. A fire in one room was quickly doused. Later, a carton containing the charred remains of several documents was sent for analysis to a team of forensic scientists.

The policemen and detectives involved in the raid were immediately shipped off along with their families on free Hawaiian vacations. Meanwhile, authorities puzzled over the evidence.

The six dead men had different countries of origin: Germany, Italy, Ireland, Syria, Lebanon and South Korea. Terrorists of various nationalities often trained together in camps in Middle Eastern countries, but this kind of international cooperation among state-sanctioned terrorists was unknown. Either they were renegades, or the bloody hydra of terrorism had once again grown a new head.

The crackpot dictators who sponsored these psychos had long vowed to spread the pernicious plague inside America's borders. The charred material found in the house in Miami proved to be maps and charts of Florida—the cities, and the waters off the coast. It looked as if the mad dogs had made their choice.

Florida was a big place. Tallahassee on the northern panhandle was closer to Atlanta than it was to Key West in the extreme south. As well as being America's vacation state and winter playground, it was also home to important military bases and major hi-tech defence- and aerospace-industry installations. No one had the slightest idea of the terrorists' specific targets. Or when they were going to strike.

Four days later, the other shoe dropped. A fourteen-person suicide squad launched an armed attack on a nuclear weapons plant in Pinellas County. They made it as far as the inner storage depot, where supplies of low-grade plutonium were kept. Security guards, many of whom had received less than a day's instruction in the use of firearms, defended the depot bravely. Many were killed. The rest retreated into the bunkers that had been built around the central storage depot as part of the plant's security arrangements. If infiltrators made it into the plant, they were to be stopped from leaving.

The arrangement worked. Seeing all chance of escape gone, the attackers set off an explosive device. Bits and pieces of thirteen bodies were spread in a wide radius over the plant grounds. A fourteenth terrorist was pulled from the ruins of the depot, barely more than a raw torso but still alive.

The Department of Energy issued a press release reporting a small contained nuclear accident, and the security guards were shipped off to join the Miami policemen in Hawaii. The last terrorist was kept alive by armed forces medical personnel long enough to give a description of one of the terrorist safehouses. It was a white stucco villa in Winter Park, a wealthy suburb built along the lakes outside Orlando.

Preparations had just begun for a raid when Barrabas and his team arrived. It was the first time the SOBs had been called in on an assignment that appeared to be entirely domestic in scope. The battle had come home to America.

The top-secret covert-action squad had been formed by a Senate subcommittee that oversaw American foreign policy. Certain objectives required measures too drastic for the niceties of diplomacy. They needed a dirty tricks team, professional soldiers who were prepared to tackle the impossible. And to die doing it if need be. The soldiers also had to be willing to do it anonymously, for the action or the money. There was to be no glory in it. If any of them were ever captured or uncovered in any way, the United States government, the military and the related intelligence agencies would deny all knowledge of their existence. The Senate committee needed mercenaries, pure, simple and illegal—someone to do the dirty work while the politicians in Washington got the credit. It was arranged for the team to receive its unofficial commission through the brokerage of an overweight Texan named Walker Jessup. The tough, highly respected former CIA operative had a reputation that had earned him the nickname The Fixer. His reputation served him well in his business as a private security consultant to anyone on the international scene who had enough bucks to pay for his exclusive services. Uncle Sam was one of his biggest clients.

After a long official career ending when he was a colonel in the Fifth Special Forces Group Airborne, Nile Barrabas had pursued a second, unofficial career as a professional soldier in mercenary wars for almost a decade. Then Jessup asked him to take on the task of recruiting and training a team. Barrabas's options at the time were severely limited. Jessup found him sharing a South American prison cell with a family of rats. The cell was too small to hold all of them, which was hardly a problem for the rats since Barrabas was about to face a firing squad.

He took the job and found the men he wanted, men who liked money and the front lines of danger. They were all a little bit psycho—not just Billy Two—a fact that hadn't escaped the attention of the Senate committee and the Senator who headed it. Nevertheless, on more than a dozen missions, they had accomplished what they set out to do against nearly impossible odds. And they came out of all the missions with their anonymity intact.

It was a good deal for a half dozen men and one woman whose temperaments, even in the best, most accommodating of worlds, would have relegated them to the fringes of normality. But it was not the best of worlds. Evil reigned incessantly seeking fertile soil in which to spread its roots, subverting humanity's most cherished values. It was a world that had need of the Soldiers of Barrabas—the SOBs.

Barrabas and his team had been brought to Florida after the debacle in Miami and the attack on the plant in Pinellas County. Initially it had been left up to state authorities to coordinate the actions of federal and state-wide law-enforcement authorities in the secret war. But pressure had built up in Washington and Tallahassee. The army and the marines wanted to move in to guard strategic military and industrial sites. However, the President was reluctant to declare martial law, which would have been necessary for the use of the armed forces as an internal police force. Barrabas and the SOBs were the radical compromise. They were given three days to strike at the terrorists before the terrorists struck. Then the President would have to decide again.

Three days and nothing to go on.

"What unit are you with?" Barrabas asked the army officer, breaking the silence in the cabin of the helicopter.

Carter's eyes snapped into focus, and he looked suspiciously at the mercenary leader. "One hundred and sixtieth." He had an accent from the deep south.

Barrabas nodded. The 160th, based in Fort Campbell, Kentucky, supplied helicopter support for antiterrorist activities. But when Barrabas had boarded, Carter had muttered something about a bumpy airplane ride from Fort Bragg, North Carolina. The young captain had a certain look about him, and Barrabas hazarded a guess he was a shooter from the U.S. Army's elite counterterrorism force, Delta. If that was the case, Carter had good reason to be unhappy.

"Used to be at Fort Bragg myself," Barrabas said quietly, to keep conversation open. He leaned back and stretched his long legs across the floor of the fuselage.

"Is that right," Carter answered, resisting further talk.

"Delta Force?"

"Not at liberty to say."

The two men rode silently for a while. Finally Major Carter spoke, embarrassed by his curt rebuff to the colonel's friendly question.

"You military?"

"Used to be. Retired. I was a colonel when I left."

"When was that?"

"After Nam."

Carter nodded, understanding the implication of the terse answer. "Your name sounded familiar when you introduced yourself. What were you doing at Bragg?"

"Special Warfare Training. My name's probably still on a few trophies in one of the mess halls. Marksmanship, and I won the three-day survival trials that year."

The captain warmed visibly. Suddenly his eyes lit up, and his unhappy face brightened. "Barrabas. I remember now. It's not the trophies. You were the last man out, weren't you? Jeez, they're still talking about you around there. Grabbing onto the skid of the helicopter as it left the roof of the U.S. Embassy in Saigon minutes before the downfall! I'm talking to the last man to leave Vietnam!"

"Well, someone had to do it," Barrabas said casually, glancing out the chopper's window at the black land mass below. An occasional light from some lonely house or anchored boat flickered on the coast. Inland, tiny headlight beams from a few cars crossing the Everglades to Miami moved through the darkness on Highway 41.

"I guess neither of us are at liberty to..."

"Nope, I guess not," Barrabas confirmed. "I just noticed that whatever the reason is that you're here, you don't look too happy about it."

The young major shifted uncomfortably and looked away, the enthusiasm of a few moments earlier fading.

"Course if we were to talk about Delta Force in generalities..." Barrabas suggested.

"That's all anyone's been doing these days, sir." Carter thought for a moment. "No harm in that, I suppose. It's not a classified unit."

With the look of someone who needed to confide, the young soldier faced the colonel. "The whole thing's pretty rocky. I mean, here's this elite unit, supposed to be made up of the best in the U.S. Army. In the trials, they put a hundred and fifty men through the toughest survival course going. You know, dumping you practically naked on the side of the mountain and saying find your way home. In the end, two of them make it onto the team. But sometimes it hasn't been the best two. It's the old-boy network. Why, a black guy still has a helluva time getting on."

Barrabas nodded. What the soldier described was hardly new to him. Nepotism—getting buddies into places of influence and prestige with little regard for real qualifications—was the kind of dry rot that was eating the U.S. military from the inside out.

"They gave us, er, the unit we're talking about? They got a new commander—from the outside, of course. A lot of guys don't like him because he uncovered a few illegalities. You know, guys skimming funds by double dipping for temporary duty pay. He's letting the disciplinary actions—even court marshals—go ahead. Not too many are happy about that. They think he should forget about it. But what else could he do? Say, 'Naughty naughty, don't do it again'? These are supposed to be the best men the army has to offer, and they got caught with their fingers in the till."

"Seems to me that Delta Force has never really been used for what it was intended."

"You got it. They sent . . . Delta Force got sent to rescue the hostages in Iran with a lot of hi-tech equipment that blew out in a simple sandstorm. Eight dead. Then they sent the Force to Grenada, where they came up with diddley squat in terms of the assigned missions. But Delta isn't an invasion force. It's a counterterrorist force. Delta's been sent out maybe a dozen or more times on terrorist actions—you know, advising the Egyptians or Maltese or whatever—but never saw action. There are some good men on that team. But, jeez, morale is like pretty much nonexistent. It's real hard going into a job when all you've tasted is..." Carter's voice faded, and he lowered his eyes.

Defeat. Barrabas knew the word, not from any armed engagement he had led, but from his experience in the military establishment. Frustration and betrayal had led to his final decision to walk and go private. Soldiering was the only profession he knew, and now he did it on his own terms. But every now and then he met a bright ambitious officer like Major Carter who was sincere in his loyalty to his unit. His heart went out to those men. They gave him hope for the fighting forces of the U.S.A.

"Major Carter..."

"Landry, sir." The young man extended his hand to shake.

Barrabas grasped it and nodded. "If there are ten more men in Delta like you, you got nothing to worry about. Victory goes to those who want it badly enough, and I can see it in your eyes."

"If we ever get a chance at it." The major's shoulders slumped and the unhappiness in his voice returned.

"What do you mean?"

"Well, all I know is the shit's about to hit the fan here in Florida. I'm supposed to get a briefing when we land and I suppose you are, too. But the law prevents the military from being used as a police force inside American borders. Only the President can change that. That means Delta's standing in line behind the local police SWATs, the National Guard and the FBI's Hostage Rescue Team. Now you bet your ass that those guys make a lot of talk about how we all train together and understand each other and how they know when to hand off and let us take over, but ..."

"Yeah, I know. Everyone's out to cover his own territory and get A plus on his report card.

Major Carter sat back in his seat and threw his hands up. "For the time being, I'm just going where I'm told to go and listening to what's spoken at me." He looked over his shoulder out the tiny helicopter window. "Say, we're going down."

There was a landing field below ringed by long low warehouses and storage depots. Several small airplanes and helicopters sat on the long tarmac. The bright lights along the perimeter of the compound illuminated the shores of a broad channel. Several long wharves extended into the waterway which ran between the mainland and some barrier islands half a mile offshore. Some men were at work on a giant hydraulic winch near a small cutter with Coast Guard markings.

The National Guard pilot brought the Bell helicopter to an easy landing on the tarmac. Nile Barrabas and the army major jumped from the cabin the moment the skids touched. They ran under the wind stream of the braking rotor as two electric-powered carts sped across the landing strip toward them.

"You didn't tell me what you've been doing since you retired from the army," Major Carter shouted to Barrabas over the noise of the chopper.

"Private operator." The two carts slowed to a halt in front of the men. "Good luck, Major."

A moment later, a taciturn driver in the uniform of the Florida National Guard whisked Barrabas smoothly across the landing strip in the direction of the wharf. He had been brought to an encampment on a man-made island that rose only a few feet above sea level. The island was almost completely surrounded by the vast wet grasslands that flowed down through southern Florida, forming the Everglades. Just beyond the eastern perimeter of buildings, the lights glared into a wall of saw grass almost twice the height of an average man. There the insects and the alligators took over. The shrill, relentless cacophony of crickets and cicadas became a force field of sound, an invisible alien wall at the edge of human settlement.

There were four metal equipment sheds with garage doors, and several smaller buildings with windows that looked like offices or bunkhouses. Overhead, above the dome formed by the lights of the camp, the night sky was cloven by the starry white swath called the Milky Way.

When they reached the wharf, the cart slowed, thudding heavily over wooden planks. A group of men wearing windbreakers was examining a dripping swimmer-delivery vehicle resting in a sling suspended from the ship's winch. Johnny Burton cast Barrabas a cool sideways glance as the merc walked up the wharf. The policeman had shaved and had traded his pretty pastel shirt for a white windbreaker with racing stripes.

The rest of them, political aides, FBI and the National Guard brass, were conferring among themselves, nodding sagely in response to each other's comments. They pointed to different features of the pod-shaped underwater craft as the cables lowered it slowly toward the pier.

The man who had summoned Barrabas to the Everglades encampment stood apart, easily recognizable from his photographs and television appearances. He was of medium height and was physically fit, and only the graying hair at his temples betrayed creeping middle age.

Although the governor of the State of Florida was deep in thought and obviously troubled, his dark intelligent eyes missed nothing.

3

Ignoring Burton and the others, Barrabas left the cart and walked slowly toward the man who would be king. The governor was in his last term, and he was pretty much a shoo-in for a Senate seat in the upcoming elections. Then there was the presidency. The American south was gaining in wealth and influence, and the Florida governor was a rising star.

Extending his hand and a warm smile, the popular political leader watched as Barrabas approached him.

"You must be Nile Barrabas. They told me I'd recognize you from your white hair."

Barrabas brushed his hand through his crewcut, a little self-consciously. "Pleased to meet you, sir," he said.

"They also told me where you got it from. A bullet in the head you took at Kap Long, which, according to medical science, should have made you a vegetable. Instead, physical trauma turned your hair white. Then there were a couple of Silver Stars and a Medal of Honor you never even showed up to collect. You're quite a hero, Mr. Barrabas. And due to the fact that you and I share a couple of secrets that none of these other men are aware of, I almost feel as if I know you personally."

"Mr. Governor, I appreciate your trust."

"Well, I appreciate fast action and fast thinking, Mr. Barrabas. Now, Mr. Walker Jessup arranged for a second truckload of weapons to be shipped down I-95, and for information about that shipment to be leaked into several terrorist networks overseas. Assuming the enemy misses the armaments we captured in Miami, they may be interested in resupplying themselves. What do you think, Mr. Barrabas. Will these terrorists go for the bait?"

"Right now, all I can tell you is that I have two of my men riding in that truck, with federal agents backing them up."

"Your best men, Mr. Barrabas?"

"All my men are the best. If there's a hijacking, they'll take care of it."

"I believe they will, Mr. Barrabas. I believe they will. And I trust you will keep me informed of any developments in that area."

"Certainly, sir."

"For the moment, I am interested in knowing how you were able to tell my people where they could find this submersible boat on the bottom of the sea. The bodies are still inside. Six of them."

"Mechanical malfunction or human error?"

The governor shrugged. "Either way, they drowned like rats in a cage. By the way, have you seen this?"

He took a folded up tabloid newspaper from under his arm. The *World Weekly News* was the kind of lurid sensational rag popular at supermarket checkout counters. This time the cover showed a blurry black-and-white photograph of a beached submersible.

Above it was the screaming headline, "Beings From Atlantis Land on Florida Beaches".

"Seems an amateur photographer got this out before we clamped the lid down. Perhaps it's one of Florida's more debatable virtues, Mr. Barrabas, but we are home to the publishing headquarters of many of these kind of newspapers."

"Must be something in the water, sir."

"In the water! Very good, Mr. Barrabas. I'll remember that. So fess up now. That was the deal as I recall. We do this in complete secrecy and if we find a submersible, you tell us how you knew it was there. Oh, by the way, we found submersibles in four of the six locations you gave us. The other three were empty."

"It was a yacht, Mr. Governor. A yacht and a computer."

The political leader raised his bushy eyebrows and threw the mercenary a look of skeptical curiosity. Barrabas had insisted on secrecy regarding the search for the submersibles in order to gain credibility for the SOBs. It was the one ace he had been dealt. Now it was time to play it and go for broke.

"A yacht and a computer, you say. Suspense builds, Mr. Barrabas."

"There's one other request that I have to make of you first, Mr. Governor."

"Another condition! Mr. Barrabas, that is not how Southern gentlemen make their deals."

"A request, Mr. Governor, not a condition. You found the submersibles, just as I said you would."

"But that is to be just a token of your sincerity? Now you have another request?"

"Yes sir."

"And what might that be?"

"Carte blanche."

"I beg your pardon."

"Carte blanche. I brought my people down here because the situation is critical. I was told to cooperate with the local authorities. So far we have. Problem is I'm an independent operator and so are my men. We don't work when we're hobbled in local red tape. I need your authority to go where I have to go, to do what has to be done without tripping over the competition, if you get my meaning."

The governor looked at him thoughtfully. "Mr. Barrabas, do you know the meaning of Florida?"

"Sir?"

"The meaning of Florida!" The politician spread his arms apart, his voice becoming boisterous. "Florida is more than just a winter playground for northern snowbirds. Hundreds of thousands of America's citizens move here to spend their retirement years, and there is a place here for every one of them, rich or poor. Leisure and recreation are the biggest industries here. You see, Florida is heaven, Mr. Barrabas. A little slice of heaven before they get the real thing. Paradise! Do you see what I'm getting at?"

"You mean trouble in paradise is bad for business."

"That's part of it. Indeed, that's part of it. What I mean, Mr. Barrabas, is that there is an innocence here, a certain freedom from the woes and tribulations of the cruel world beyond the borders of this state. Perhaps this is an illusion, but if so, it is one that many of our citizens have worked their entire lives for. This is what Florida means to America. We cannot afford to lose that innocence, Mr. Barrabas. Heaven must remain inviolate or the myth will be destroyed forever.''

The governor gestured toward the submersible, which swung slightly as the winch's cables smoothly uncoiled. The two men began to walk slowly along the pier as he continued to talk.

''I've been informed there are problems between you and Mr. Burton of the state attorney general's office. Apparently your people find it difficult to take prisoners for questioning. Of course, competition is what our society stands for in the marketplace, though I can see it might create difficulties elsewhere.''

''No one could have taken those terrorists for questioning, Mr. Governor. For one thing, it was a suicide squad. For another... ''

The submersible settled on the pier with a thud and a sudden relaxing of the sling. Coast Guard sailors jumped to unhook the cables that held the fiberglass pod to the winch. Bloated decomposing bodies could be seen through the condensation on the Plexiglas hood, their eyeless faces staring nowhere. A cruel smell emanated from the underwater coffin, forcing Burton and the others who were nearby to beat a hasty retreat.

A tall older man with a short white moustache and silver hair turned from the crowd and sauntered over to the governor.

''Roger Davies,'' he introduced himself to Barrabas with a broad friendly smile and his hand extended. ''I'm an old friend of Bob's,'' he explained, looking affectionately at the governor.

"And my campaign manager," the politician added.

"Past, present and future," said Davies, grinning and taking a cigar from his breast pocket. "Cigar? Don't mind if I do," he said, answering his own question and striking a lighter. As an afterthought, he produced another cigar and offered it to Barrabas. The colonel accepted, bit off one end and held the other to the flame of the lighter.

"He don't smoke," Davies said, nudging his friend and candidate, with a wink of complicity at Barrabas.

"Well, now that you two are puffing smoke like a couple of factories in violation of my air pollution statutes," the governor joked, "why don't we go over to my current headquarters. I believe we have a great deal to discuss."

He turned to the men who were still eyeing the submersible from a distance. Two of them donned white plastic jump suits and pulled on rubber gloves in preparation for the opening of the underwater craft and the gruesome task that lay ahead. "Gentlemen!" the governor called. "We are ready."

Johnny Burton and the remaining men, including Major Landry Carter, began to walk down the pier, following them toward the smaller buildings on the eastern side of the camp.

"Am I allowed to know where I am?" Barrabas asked as they crossed the compound.

"Why you surely are, Mr. Barrabas. This here's a secret base camp used by Florida law enforcement authorities. The game wardens use it when they go after alligator poachers, and the Coast Guard uses it when they're rounding up drug smugglers. My people tell me that with all the night activity here right now, it won't be secret much longer."

They passed one of the equipment sheds near the perimeter of the encampment. Beside it, three good-sized alligators in a mud slough were tied to wooden stakes with stout ropes. The alligators strained at their bonds and snapped angrily at the men who stopped briefly to watch them.

"Camp mascots," explained the governor. He pointed past the perimeter of the camp. "Ten yards from here, the Everglades are crawling with them. When they crawl up here, they get enlisted."

"Bobby gives me the same line he gave you, Mr. Barrabas, that this camp is used by the law." Roger Davies's eyes twinkled with humor. "I think he's hoodwinking us and it's really his own secret private hunting camp to which I and none of my friends have ever been invited."

He picked up a long stick from the ground and prodded the nearest beast. The angry alligator snapped and leaped forward until the rope strained and yanked it back. Roger Davies poked the giant reptile again. This time it slithered back into the mud slough and eyed the older man with reptilian contempt, its yellow-edged pupils glowing in the dark.

"Sizing us up for dinner, I'd say." Rogers threw the stick into the slough. The alligator snapped at him once again before scrambling around on its short legs and turning its back.

"Roger keeps trying to persuade me to do some gator hunting with him, just like when I was a kid." The good-natured governor began moving toward one of the smaller buildings in the compound. "I can't seem to get it through to him that I am now the governor of this state and charged with protecting its endangered species, not killing them."

"Endangered my ass," Davies muttered. "Why these days, the gators come right up on the golf course at Palm Beach, eating puppy dogs and little babies."

At the door, the governor waved Barrabas and Davies ahead of him. They entered a rustic, wood-panelled room lined with steel cots. The walls were covered with topographical and nautical maps interspersed with a few yellowed pinups from a popular girlie magazine. One side of the room was dominated by a short-wave radio, and six metal bunk beds stood against the other side. A long table lined with chairs ran down the center of the room. An expensive leather briefcase sat on one end of the table, and a yellow legal-sized notepad and a single sharpened pencil were carefully positioned at each seat.

"Informal, but adequate," the governor commented, heading toward the chair near the briefcase. "Please, be seated." He motioned Barrabas to sit beside him at the head of the table. "The others will be here in a moment. I want them in on this."

The door opened. The five men from the pier entered and filed toward chairs at the long table. With the exception of Johnny Burton and Major Landry Carter, they were big solid men in their forties and fifties. All of them moved with the wary self-confidence of veteran law enforcement officers.

"As you all know, this man has been lent to us by Washington on condition that the agency he represents remain classified," the governor began, point-

ing to Barrabas. "Now, I don't like that any more than
you do, but I did agree to that condition, and as a
Southerner and a gentlemen, I'll hold to my word.
Perhaps y'all can take time to introduce yourselves."

Each man around the table spoke in turn.

"Forest McIvor, FBI, Miami Investigative Divi-
sion and unit leader of the Hostage Rescue Team."

"Major Landry Carter, Delta Force."

"Axel Joe Douglasson, representing the Florida
National Guard, the finest in the USA."

"Noah Breaker. My affiliation is classified and not
relevant here."

"Oh, pshaw!" Roger Davies spat out impatiently.
"He's CIA and we all know it. And I understand
you've already met Johnny Burton, Mr. Barrabas.
He's been appointed as central liaison between the
state attorney general's office, this committee and the
local police SWAT teams across the state. Give us the
breakdown, Johnny."

Burton picked up a pencil lying on the table and
tapped it against the blank notepad in front of him as
he spoke. "All local, county and state police forces are
on alert, as well as the National Guard. All leaves have
been cancelled. In conjunction with Axel Joe Douglasson, and using units of the National Guard, we've
beefed up security at all defence-industry installations, nuclear facilities, the space center and military
installations. We've done the same at airports, train
stations and in the major port facilities in Tampa,
Miami and everywhere else. So far, we've been able to
keep a lid on why, and because the coordinating has
been done through me, none of the forces involved are

fully aware of the extent of the mobilization. But there are rumors."

"Mr. McIvor, can you give us a report on your agency's activities?" the governor asked the FBI man.

"Certainly. We've moved in several hundred agents, including hostage rescue teams from other states. These units have been distributed throughout Florida. We're in the process of questioning every person in the state with known or suspected connections to radical political or nationalist movements. There are thousands of them, especially in the Miami area. It's not going to be easy, but we're used to that kind of work. We'll hit them one by one, and somewhere along the way, one of them is going to give us something."

"Have you got anything right now, though?" Davies taunted. "That's what we want to know."

McIvor cleared his throat. "Er, not since the unsuccessful raid on the villa at Winter Park. Our agents are still there, searching for—"

"So in other words, except for these submersibles that Mr. Barrabas managed to find, we're no farther ahead than we were a week ago," Davies said angrily.

There was an uncomfortable silence around the table. The governor sat back and looked around the table, his face a mask

Major Carter quietly spoke. "If I may say so, we are at least better prepared if and when the terrorists do strike. And, as the governor knows, the President has already ordered all military counterterrorism units to Florida on standby."

There were gasps from McIvor and Burton.

Barrabas spoke up. "It seems to me there's an emphasis on protecting military and industrial installations and some of the traditional targets of terrorism like the airports. What about places where people just gather?"

"What do you mean?" Davies demanded sharply.

Barrabas shrugged. "Terrorists demand publicity. A good way to get that is to slaughter people. Now if I were a terrorist, and I were coming to Florida, I'd go where the people go."

"Tourist sites," Major Carter concluded.

"There are hundreds of them! Why—" Roger Davies slapped the flat of his hand on the table "—there's no way we can guard them unless we bring in the army and declare martial law!"

"Only the President can do that, and that will not happen unless I am consulted," the governor said sternly. "And until then, gentlemen, I am in charge. Mr. Breaker has some preliminary information for us on the origins of the swimmer delivery vehicles, as I believe they are called."

Visibly pleased to be called upon, the secret agent drew a small notebook from his shirt pocket and flipped it open. He read from his notes. "They were built by one of our major defence department contractors two years ago and shipped to Turkey as part of its routine NATO consignments. Four months later, they were declared obsolete and sold as surplus on the open market."

"Four months later!" the major from Delta Force exclaimed. "Sounds to me like an appropriations scandal brewing somewhere in the Turkish military."

"It might be interesting to know who signed the papers declaring them obsolete," Forest MacIvor pointed out.

"Oh, they were definitely obsolete. Replaced four years ago by safer, more reliable models," Noah Breaker said. "We're trying to find out why the submersibles were shipped in the first place."

"What's the name of the contractor who built them?" Barrabas asked.

The CIA agent consulted his notes again. "Name? Gorgon Incorporated. Based in Maryland."

Roger Davies narrowed his eyes and addressed the colonel. "Now, that was quite some trick of yours, Mr. Barrabas, knowing where we could find those little bitty boat things out there on the sea bottom. We are most anxious to learn how you did it."

"Our people have been looking for a break for a week now," Axel Joe Douglasson exclaimed with obvious resentment. "And twenty-four hours after you're brought in—not without substantial opposition from our own people, I might add—you manage to come up with the locations of these here submersible crafts that have been bringing these terrorists ashore. Now either you've got some information we don't have, or we figure you're working for them."

The governor signaled his displeasure with the National Guardsman's last comment. He turned to Barrabas. "Now earlier you were saying something about a yacht and a computer."

"Yes, sir." The colonel shifted uncomfortably, flicking his eyes around the table and watching the other men carefully. "When we arrived, we requested all the Coast Guard records on marine traffic for the last two weeks. One of my men computerized them and did a match up with the submersibles that had been found a week ago."

"But those submersibles were released from ships far out at sea!" Forest McIvor of the FBI asserted.

"That was a theory," Barrabas rejoined. "Not necessarily fact. We found several boats that were recorded in the general area of the submersibles at a time consistent with their landings. Elimination was easy. Most were too small. We were left with one major suspect—a hundred-foot yacht. We charted its progress down the east coast of Florida, around the Keys and up the Gulf coast. Using speed averages we were able to figure out roughly where it dropped anchor each night over a two-week period. Those are the coordinates we gave you."

Johnny Burton threw his pencil angrily onto the table. "You son of a bitch. You've been holding out...."

"Gentlemen!" Roger Davies interjected. "May I remind you all of the seriousness of the situation and of the company present." He nodded toward the governor.

"Where is this yacht now?" Noah Breaker demanded. "And what's the registration on it? If its foreign ..."

"Sorry to disappoint you, Noah, but the CIA will have to take a rain check. The registration is Virginia. And for the last twenty-four hours it's been at anchor just off Tampa Bay—under surveillance by my men."

Forest McIvor huffed, obviously disgruntled. "You had a duty, Mr. Barrabas, to inform the FBI—"

"Gentlemen!" Roger Davies said sharply.

Barrabas looked quickly at the governor, who was shrewdly holding back. It was obvious that Roger Davies was more than an old friend and campaign manager. He was the governor's loyal, right-hand man and enjoyed the politician's total confidence. The type of man who was a necessary fixture in any political organization, Davies was undoubtedly the man the governor relied on to carry out unpleasant tasks. Barrabas suspected that Davies's aggressiveness at the meeting had been well rehearsed in advance and that the governor would come in with the final word.

"And how many other secret projects have you got on the go, Mr. Barrabas?" the CIA man asked coolly.

"I think we can avoid suspicion and recrimination, gentlemen." The governor glanced quickly at Barrabas, his eyes carefully veiled. "Mr. Barrabas verified his activities with me personally before acting on them. He should be commended for some excellent sleuthing. I understand your feelings, but we must, all of us, continue to work together."

"Someone's got to hit that yacht," Douglasson pointed out.

"Indeed. The organizations and agencies that each of you represent all have specific assigned responsibilities. We will continue to coordinate them through this committee and my office. Mr. Barrabas and his people will take care of the yacht. They are to have the fullest cooperation from each of you. If there is a jurisdictional dispute, bring it to me. If there is insufficient time to bring it to me, it is to be resolved in favor of Mr. Barrabas and his people. Are there any questions?"

Chastened, the men at the table looked at each other. Axel Joe Douglasson spoke up.

"If that's what the governor of Florida wants, that's good enough for me, sir."

"If there's nothing else, you gentlemen are dismissed. I suggest we all get some sleep before we're completely useless. You are welcome to make use of the facilities here, primitive as they are, or the helicopters will taxi you back to your respective headquarters. Mr. Barrabas, I'd like to discuss the matter of the yacht with you further."

Barrabas, the governor and Roger Davies remained behind as the other men filed out. When the door closed, Davies rubbed his hands together.

"Well, that sure got the mullet jumping, didn't it, Bob?" the politician's friend cackled. "And, Mr. Barrabas, that was mighty interesting information about that yacht. You deserve to be congratulated."

The politician looked at the colonel. "I'm not giving you carte blanche, Mr. Barrabas, but I'm going to let you take a leadership role. In other words, I want you to do what you think's necessary, but I want you to clear it with me first. Is that understood?"

Barrabas nodded slowly. "As long as events don't outpace us."

"I hear what you're saying, but may I remind you that it's your job to make sure that they don't. Remember the conditions of your employment. No one knows who you are, where you come from or why you're here. As far as the law is concerned—and to those men who just left, the law is what I tell them it is—you and your people are private operators working on your own and committing enough crimes to put you all in the slammer for the rest of your lives. If not in the electric chair. Got that?"

"It's the way we've always worked, sir."

"But normally outside the country, as I understand it. The ramifications of your actions inside America's borders might well be . . . more serious. Is my meaning clear?"

"It's clear."

"Good, because whatever these terrorists are planning is bound to be bloody. I need someone who can go in there and kick ass like it's never been kicked before. The rest of the guys who were here all have constitutional and other legal restrictions on their authority. The only limitation you have is the level of risk you're personally prepared to accept. Now what about this yacht?"

"All we needed was something to corroborate our suspicions. We have that now—out there on the pier, full of dead men."

"Can your people take it?"

"Yes, sir, we can."

"Then take it. Report back to me when it's done. And keep me informed of the progress of our fishing expedition on I-95."

"Fishing expedition? What's that?" Davies asked quickly, looking from the governor to the colonel.

"Oh, another one of Mr. Barrabas's secrets, Roger," the governor replied. "That's all, Mr. Barrabas."

The mercenary leader pushed back his chair and stood, his six feet plus towering over the politician and his campaign manager. "We won't let you down, Mr. Governor."

The politician looked up at him for a moment. "No, sir, I don't believe you will."

The two Floridians stayed seated until Barrabas had left. The governor sighed deeply.

"What d'ya think of all that, Roger?" he asked his old friend and political confidant.

The older, white-haired man shook his head pensively. "I think you handled it just fine, Bobby. Helluva thing to happen in an election year, that's for sure."

"Yep. And I'll come out of it one of two ways—smelling like roses with the Senate seat, maybe even the presidency, sewn up, or with my career destroyed. No, sir, there ain't no in-between on this one."

"And that there hotheaded mercenary young fellow. What if he fouls up on you? What you going to do about that?"

The governor looked at his friend, trying to read what was behind the older man's eyes. He saw it, but he asked anyway.

"What would you do, Roger?"

"The gators, Bobby. The gators."

"I admire him. He's a dedicated man, brave as hell to be operating outside the law. But you're right, Roger. If it ever comes down to his neck or mine, I don't have a choice."

"You think he don't know that?"

Florida's favorite son pondered the question for a moment. "He knows. That's what makes him the best man I've got for the job ahead of us. He plays to win because he's gotta. If he doesn't, he'll be thrown to the wolves."

"To the gators, Bob."

"Wolves or gators, Roger, it won't make much difference," the governor concluded. "Either way, he gets eaten alive."

4

At the entrance to Tampa Bay, the warm Gulf waters swirling past Anna Maria Key were deceptive, concealing treachery in the powerful currents beneath the surface. With the unceasing rhythm of the earth's oldest melody, breakers kissed the sandy beaches of Egmont Key, a few miles to the north.

The cities of St. Petersburg and Clearwater, several miles beyond, formed a single orange dome over the low dark mass of the Sun Coast. Much farther away, across more than thirty miles of water, the port of Tampa shone into the night sky. In the southeast there was Bradenton, the orange-juice capital of eastern Florida. The lights of American civilization glittered, tropical diamonds on the black velvet night.

Headlights of cars arced gracefully over the old Sunshine Skyway, the slender causeway and bridge that spanned the eight miles between the northern and the southern shores of Tampa Bay.

"Kind of gives you the creeps, doesn't it?" Alex "the Greek" Nanos reached over the side of the power cruiser. He swatted the crest of a dark wave as it rocked against the boat.

"What's that?" Geoff Bishop lowered a pair of light-sensitive binoculars and leaned against the helm.

"Just knowing these waters are full of hungry momma sharks. Hell, they think we're nothing more than gourmet snacks for their kids." He wiped his hand on his pants and rested it on the steering wheel of the fifty-foot Italian motorboat.

"What makes you think we're gourmet? To a shark, fresh meat triggers an instinct that pounds its primeval imperative into its tiny brain."

"Big words confuse me, Geoff," Nanos replied. He slapped his hand impatiently against the steering wheel. "Goddamn sharks. I could go for a swim right now. Goddamn sharks and goddamn terrorists. Say, what's happening over there?"

Bishop shook his head. "Nothing. Absolutely nothing." He raised the binoculars to his eyes again and gazed at the lights of a hundred-foot yacht anchored about a mile north of them. The running lights on the high sleek hull and the soft yellow glow from the curtained staterooms shone on the rippled waves of the Gulf. The boat was silent. Occasionally the figure of a man standing on the deck smoking a cigarette could be seen.

The mercs had been keeping the yacht under surveillance for almost twenty-four hours, and they were almost prepared to throw in the towel.

They were aboard a sleek Italian-designed cruiser that had originally been built for a tall sports fisherman who craved luxury. The small but elegantly appointed staterooms below deck had more than six feet of headroom. And in the cockpit, there was a cooler the size of a steamer trunk for keeping fish cool. It looked as if it had never been used.

The decisive factor in choosing the boat was its speed. Despite the cruiser's size, with her high-powered Italian engines, she could do more than sixty miles an hour open throttle. The high-performance cruiser also provided an excellent cover. If anyone on the yacht returned surveillance, all they'd see was a couple of wealthy fishermen in a half-million-dollar boat anchored just off Anna Maria Key. Sitting aboard the cruiser was hardly a hardship job, but the sheer boredom of waiting for something to happen was mind numbing. And Barrabas had tagged them together on the assignment despite the fact that neither merc particularly enjoyed the other's company.

"Speaking of sharks, there are a couple of them swimming about a hundred and fifty feet off the boat right now," Bishop said, following the sharks' movements with the binoculars.

"What!" Nanos lurched forward in his seat, his right hand slipping inside his windbreaker. His instinct was to reach for a gun.

"Cool it, Alex. It's just a momma shark and a daddy shark heading for Tampa Bay to make babies. They're straight off the bow."

"Give me those." Nanos took the binoculars and put them to his eyes. "Yeah, them and about a million other sharks who come here from the South Atlantic to breed. What makes Tampa Bay so popular?" He adjusted the focus and scanned the dark waves in front of the boat until he saw the two black triangular fins cutting the water like the tips of knives. "Whewww! Big momma and poppa shark!"

"If it's any comfort, there are probably just as many sharks of the two-legged kind on land in Florida. As long as we stay in the boat, the fish won't bite us."

The Greek gave Geoff Bishop a baleful stare. "Being cooped up in a motor cruiser with you isn't my idea of a good time." He shoved the light-sensitive binoculars at the Canadian airman and fell back in his seat, folding his arms stubbornly across his chest.

"So? Swim," Bishop said, outlining the Greek's choices succinctly.

The longstanding enmity between Barrabas's two mercs had subsided considerably over the time they had worked for Barrabas, but lingering resentment still surfaced occasionally. Bishop, a decorated veteran of the Canadian Air Force, had been brought on to the team as an expert helicopter pilot. The SOBs' first pilot, Al Chen, bought a one-way ticket to the sky during a deadly mission in Iran.

Bishop was the new boy, and Alex Nanos never let him forget it. A further complication was the physical attraction between the airman and Lee Hatton, which had blossomed into an on-again, off-again affair.

Nanos had been born with a volatile temper and recognized early in life that his two main talents were fighting and womanizing. Often he did both at the same time. After joining the U.S. Coast Guard, he'd discovered his third talent, navigating. He was known to brag, not without justification, that if someone put a propeller on an orange crate, he could sail it to China.

Unfortunately, the handsome, dark-haired Greek's penchant for mouthing off at his superior officers and for going AWOL to spend time in the arms of buxom babes had brought his career as the Coast Guard's finest navigator to an end. He'd hooked up with a former Marine commando, an American Indian named Billy Starfoot II. For a while, the two men had terrorized the fleshpots of Miami as well paid gigolos. Eventually Barrabas had found them. The Greek had been given another chance and something real to fight for.

Nanos handed the binoculars back to Bishop.

"Why do you suppose the colonel keeps putting us together on assignments?"

Bishop waited a moment, scanning the yacht again before answering.

"Because we don't like each other."

There was a long silence in the boat. Nanos sighed. Sometimes he felt like a jackass, and he knew he deserved to. He was still ashamed of— Never mind, he thought. He was too ashamed to bring it up. And in front of everyone, too.

"You feel that way?" he asked, disingenuous to the end.

Bishop lowered the binoculars and looked at the Greek. Rubbing his chin with his hand—the chin Nanos had slugged in a bar in Thailand not long ago— Bishop said, "What d'ya expect? If you weren't working for the Colonel, too, I'd have... Never mind."

"You'd have what?" Nanos was suddenly alert. He looked at Bishop with a slight smile.

Bishop shook his head.

"C'mon, what? A good old knock-'em-down, all-out, fist-fighting brawl? Hey, might have done us both good."

Now it was Bishop's turn to look at Nanos. "What d'ya mean?"

"To get it out of our systems. I don't know why I got on your case, Geoff. Maybe because of that thing you have going with Lee. It seemed like you moved in on her so fast, right after you came aboard as one of the team."

"Lee makes her own decisions."

Alex nodded. "I know that."

"And you know something, Alex? I'm not part of the team. At least, not as far as you're concerned. You've always tried to shut me out."

"You felt that way?" The Greek was genuinely surprised.

"Sure."

"You've covered my ass a few times, you know, when the bullets started flying and it looked like our chances of getting out of someplace were smaller than a snowman's in Florida."

"Yup. And I will again when I have to. But when I work with you, I'm working alone. It's like I save your ass because if push comes to shove, I want you there to save mine. Enlightened self-interest I think it's called. It's not like that when I'm on assignment with the other guys. When I'm working with Billy Two, or Claude or Liam, then I feel like, well, we're working together. Really together, you know. All for one and one for all, as they say. I don't feel that way with you."

Alex Nanos sat silently for a few moments, looking at Tampa Bay, at the lights of the cities and at the yacht floating gently on the water.

"It's just about your turn with these," Bishop said, raising the binoculars to his eyes. "It's almost midnight. I have to go below and radio a report into Nate. Maybe the colonel will have something else for us to do by now. I hope so."

"Geoff?"

"Yeah?"

"I'm sorry."

The Greek's words caught Geoff Bishop off guard.

"What?"

"I'm sorry. For all the trouble. For the hassles." Alex moved his hand away from the steering wheel and held it out to Bishop. "Let's start being a team."

Bishop looked at Nanos's hand, then at the Greek's face, for a moment unsure, and unable to conceal his surprise.

"A team." He nodded. "Sure."

They shook.

"Here, your turn," Bishop shoved the binoculars at the Greek and stepped down from the bridge to go below. Then he heard a faint droning in the distance.

"Awright!" Nanos exclaimed. "When this is over with, I'm going to throw a party for you and me that will blow Florida away."

Bishop stepped back up, his ears alert to the steady sound of an approaching high-speed motor.

"Alex, give me those." He took the binoculars from Nanos's hands.

"Daytona Beach, Fort Lauderdale—hell, we'll rip through the coast from Key West to Jacksonville Beach! Geoff?"

Bishop stood almost at attention, gazing steadily through the field glasses toward Egmont Key. A small green running light skimmed across the dark water toward the yacht.

Nanos whistled and murmured in disbelief. "Something's happening."

There was activity aboard the yacht, too. On the deck below the bridge, bright lights blinked on. Three men left the forward stateroom and stood by the side, waiting to receive the visiting boat.

"What is it?" Nanos asked Bishop.

"There are three men on the deck and two in the motorboat. One of them is . . . Damn!"

"What's the matter?"

"It's the currents here, swinging us one way and the yacht the other. I can't see what's going on anymore."

"Then let's get closer."

Nanos flicked the switch that automatically reeled in the anchor, then pushed the ignition button.

"Bad idea!" Bishop said. "If they see us suddenly moving across the water, they'll be . . ."

"We'll keep the lights out." The five-fifty-horsepower engines grumbled hesitantly, then kicked into action.

"Yeah, but I think it'd be better to go farther into the bay where we could intercept the speedboat." The pulsating rhythm of the engines hummed through the fiberglass hull of the cruiser.

"In this thing!" Alex slipped the gear into drive and edged the throttle forward. "Geoff, next time we're in an airplane, you say jump, and I'm gone. But on this ship, I'm the navigator, like captain, you know. We're just going to slip along the shore like we're looking for fish, and we'll curve in a little closer while we're doing it. What are they going to do to us? Blow us out of the water?"

Bishop glanced at his watch. They still had twenty minutes before the radio transmission to Nate Beck was due.

He felt incredibly exposed on the water. Sitting ducks. No cover and nowhere to hide. In the air, a man could engage the enemy and go anywhere—up, down, forward, backward or sideways on any conceivable angle. The only limitation on movement was the design of the aircraft. And then there was speed. He glanced at the roiling sea trail the motors churned up as the fifty-foot boat pushed forward. He would never get over the feeling that, in a fight, a boat was a slow-moving death trap.

Several minutes passed before Nanos was able to steer into an angle that allowed Bishop a view of the bridge. The men on the deck of the yacht were clearly illuminated. One wore a business suit and glasses. Another one wore dark pants and a bulky windbreaker. Bishop guessed he was the man who had climbed up from the speedboat. A third man, dressed in casual white pants and a short-sleeved white shirt, stood with his hands in his pockets.

The man in the windbreaker gesticulated wildly as he talked. The man in white listened, unruffled. He turned to the third man and spoke. Abruptly the men turned and disappeared through the open door of the stateroom. The bright exterior lights went out.

Bishop felt something harden in the pit of his stomach. There was still a man sitting in the speedboat, which was hidden from their view on the other side of the yacht. It didn't make sense. He adjusted the binoculars. The small quantities of light available were automatically amplified by an electronic intensifier system that adjusted the image for light sensitivity.

"What's happening?" Nanos asked from the wheel.

"I dunno."

The lights in the main stateroom went out, and the door opened. Two men carrying a heavy square box came out. They set the box on the deck and leaned over to adjust something.

"How far away are we now?"

"A little more than a klick. Maybe three quarters of a mile. If the jig is up, we can still outrun them and their bullets."

Suddenly a blinding light seared across the lenses of the binoculars, causing Bishop to yank them from his eyes. He and Alex were bathed in milky whiteness, seized by a brilliant yellow eye that had blinked open on the deck of the yacht.

"A spot!" Alex shouted as the two mercs reached for the automatic rifles in the helm.

The luxury motorboat blew out from underneath them, throwing the two men into a maelstrom of exploding debris. Concussion waves from the missile blast swatted them into the air. Heat waves followed, then a roar as the Italian cruiser erupted under a fountain of flame spewing from the water.

Fire seared the side of his body and shards of fi-
breglass lacerated his skin as Geoff Bishop flopped
through the air. His limbs seemed to tear from their
sockets. He saw flames burning up the side of his
clothing, felt himself losing consciousness. He must
have fought it, because suddenly he was aware of an
opening in the vortex of fire and debris.

He curled, closing his arms about his head, and hit
the water like a burning cannonball, sizzling as his
momentum drove him far beneath the surface. The
seawater closed around him like a glove, snuffing the
flames, the water's coolness filling his head with a
sudden clarity. He spread his arms and legs, arresting
his downward movement. He brought his arms to his
sides, then slid them forward and kicked. He had no
air. Like a wire being stretched tight between his temples, a scream built within him.

He ordered himself not to breath, froze his lungs,
his throat, and forced his tongue back in his mouth to
shut the air passage to his nose. His arms swept back
and his legs kicked, his muscles crying, begging for
more oxygen. The scream in his head tightened, grew
louder, descended his vertebrae. He felt himself uri-
nating, his vision spotted with gunpowder, fading, the
scream dying.

He hit cool air.

His mouth opened, and he gasped, the air ripping
into empty lungs. Water caught in his throat, and a
cough hacked through his body, forcing the air out.
His body sank. A cruel wave smashed into his face and
sped away.

Don't breath, he ordered himself. With his remaining strength he pulled toward the surface. Again he

broke the surface. Keeping his mouth shut and his head high, he drank the sweet air, filling his chest. Burning wreckage from the boat floated around him and cast eerie orange reflections along the tar-black water. Alex. Where was Alex?

Painfully white light began to flood his peripheral vision. The spotlight on the yacht was coldly ferreting for survivors. Holding air in, Bishop pulled himself under the water once again. The burning flotsam illuminated the water for several feet in places, and the spotlight from the yacht seared a long trail into the blue-green depths. It was either a dim recollection of the first few seconds after the missile hit or an urgent gut feeling, but somehow Bishop knew Alex Nanos had been thrown over the side of the powerboat away from the yacht.

He swam from the spotlight and surfaced for air on the far side of a large floating object. The bathtub-sized cooler from the ship's cockpit had escaped the explosion unscathed. It shielded him perfectly from the penetrating white beam. He grabbed it and held on for a moment's rest, while he turned and surveyed the wreckage swirling over the water.

No Nanos. The yacht's engines rumbled through the water, and the hundred-foot boat slid forward. The spotlight tracked back and forth through the night. Some debris floated in darkness thirty feet away. Bishop pulled himself forward in a quiet but powerful breast stroke, desperately conscious that each passing second lessened the chances of finding Nanos alive.

He treaded water, turning madly to scan for some sign of the missing man. His leg kicked something under the surface. He flipped and dived. His hand felt flesh—a body sinking slowly downward.

The search was over.Bishop kicked deeper, opening and closing both hands until one of them grasped a limb. He propelled himself upward, pulling the unconscious body with him. As he approached the surface, he used both hands to push Nanos ahead of him toward precious, life-giving air.

The Greek's head broke the surface and lolled back. His eyes were closed. He wasn't breathing. His shirt had been blown away from his chest, and blood oozed into the water from a fist-sized wound just below his shoulder and clavicle.

Bishop hooked his left arm under Alex's armpits and behind him, forcing Alex's limp head to rest against his forearm. Kicking his legs to keep them both above water, the Canadian airman pushed his index finger into Alex's mouth. Seawater poured out. Bishop thrust his legs together, forcing himself high out of the water. As he came down, he planted his mouth firmly around Nanos's and exhaled.

The air popped from Alex's mouth as Bishop sank back into the water. The drowned man's windpipe was blocked. Gasping for breath, the Canadian flipped Nanos forward and slammed the heel of his hand into the small of Nanos's back. He forced the unconscious man onto his back again. Supporting Alex's torso with one arm, Geoff Bishop held the Greek's head back. Once again he kicked hard, sealing his lips around Nanos's mouth and breathing into him.

Alex's chest rose in the water. Bishop took his mouth away, sucked in a lungful of air and breathed into Nanos again. For a second time, the man's chest rose and fell. Bishop tried again, unconscious of his own ebbing strength, impelled by the knowledge that Alex's life was ticking rapidly away.

Nanos jerked. A cough caught in his throat. Bishop felt the Greek's body floating away as Nanos's lungs filled with air. They rose halfway and stopped. Bishop strained to catch his breath. Once again he held Nanos's head back and exhaled his air into the Greek's mouth.

He took his mouth away and felt the breath escape. Then Nanos breathed in, quickly respirating a short gasp of air. His lungs caught again, and another breath of air hissed from his mouth. Cradling the unconscious man's body in his arms, Bishop felt the rise and fall of Nanos's chest as he began to breathe regularly. Then suddenly the steady rhythmic pounding of the man's heart thudded in his unconscious body.

The airman lay back in the water, holding Nanos across his chest with one arm and sculling gently with the other. The yacht seemed to have given up the search. The spotlight still trailed along the water but at some distance from the smoldering debris. The lights along the shores of Tampa Bay twinkled seductively in the forbidding distance.

Alone, Bishop knew he could make it, although it would take him until morning. With an unconscious man, he didn't know. But if he failed, it wouldn't be for want of trying. The immediate problem, he realized, was Alex's wound. If he ripped his shirt, he could stuff the man's wound and tie it down. One way or another, he had to stop the bleeding.

Blood.

The word stopped in Bishop's mind. He remembered.

Blood attracted sharks.

The airman looked up and saw them barely thirty feet away. Silhouetted against light on the yacht, the dagger tips of two dorsal fins cut slowly through the waves of Tampa Bay, drawn by the fresh scent of human prey.

5

Lee Hatton gazed through the windows of the twentieth floor suite toward MacDill Air Force Base and the great dark rim of Tampa Bay beyond. The lights of St. Petersburg formed a dim yellow halo on the far horizon where the bay opened into the Gulf of Mexico. Less than a mile away, the perimeter fences of the air base were visible under bright arc lights, and the long straight lines of the runways were neatly marked with blue flashers.

Another F-13 came in for a night landing, ferrying its secret cargo of highly trained antiterrorist troops from Kentucky and South Carolina. If news of the terrorist threat and the military buildup became public, there would be carnage on the interstate highways leading north as millions of panicking tourists drove over each other in their flight to safety.

The penthouse suite occupied the twentieth story of a building that had been built for married officers from MacDill air base. Until recently, the suite had been the dream home of a general, but then he'd quietly retired after certain irregularities in multimillion dollar defence contracts were brought to his attention. The entire suite, which sprawled across the top floor of the building, with views in all directions, had been requisitioned and transformed into a temporary command headquarters for the SOBs. What had once been a living room was now lined with a long row of computers, communication equipment, modems, monitors, scramblers and sophisticated electronic tracking devices. Nate Beck, the SOBs' computer and electronic communications expert, sat in a padded chair at the center of the system.

There was no doubt that Beck, a diminutive Jewish New Yorker, was a brilliant hacker. His early career, developing secret codes in U.S. army intelligence, had proved it. Later, in private industry, he had designed some of the earliest applications of microchips. Despite his pivotal role in the development of the revolutionary new technology and perhaps because he met each challenge as soon as it was presented to him, he had become bored with his work.

With a lust typical of a man who worked so many hours at a desk, he had craved action and adventure. He'd lost himself in a fantasy world and had come up with a scheme for the perfect robbery.

His computer scam had raked nickels and dimes out of millions of bank accounts until the balance in his own account had hit seven digits. Then he'd withdrawn the money and fled to Switzerland. He might have gotten away with it if his wife hadn't informed on him. Barrabas had reached Beck's refuge in an Alpine hotel with a recruitment offer minutes before Interpol had arrived.

The installation of the elaborate computer, communications and tracking systems in the SOBs' makeshift command post was something Barrabas had demanded as a condition of the SOBs' employment.

Barrabas didn't trust the army or civilian intelligence agencies to give him what he needed as fast as he wanted it. There was too much professional jealousy from the likes of Johnny Burton.

On the walls over the banks of cables and electronic equipment, maps of the United States, the state of Florida and Florida's major cities had been carefully laid out. Red circles marked the location of military bases, defence department installments, vital warning systems, strategic energy supply lines as well as the private industrial plants that were Defense Department contractors. Florida industrialists manufactured everything from toilet seats to Star Wars laser devices for the Pentagon.

Lee Hatton moved the names of the cities silently over her tongue: Miami, Palm Beach, Boca Raton, Fort Lauderdale, Coconut Grove. The words alone held much of the exotic allure of the tropical state.

"Hey, Nate!" Hatton called. "What's the word from Geoff and Alex?"

"They're due to report in a few minutes. Never fear, Lee. You'll be the first to know."

"Don't do me any favors."

"Who's doing you a favor? Just so's you'll stop asking every five minutes. Is it Bishop or just boredom?"

"Give me a break. Besides, whatever's going on between Geoff and I is, one, private and, two, totally on hold the minute we're put on assignment. And don't forget it." She sank back in an overstuffed chair and yanked one of her boots off. Moaning with pleasure, she twisted her foot and wriggled her toes.

"Mmmmm, that feels good." She leaned forward to start on the laces of the other boot. "I should just take a hint from you, Billy, and forget about wearing them altogether."

The big Indian sat nearby, his arms folded across his massive chest, his mouth an even, impassive line under dark eyes and a heavy brooding brow. He gazed silently out the window at the lights of a helicopter approaching in the distance. At the mention of his name he turned toward the woman.

"Hmph," he grunted doubtfully. "I follow the wisdom of Hawk Spirit," he said, referring to his ancestral Osage warrior god. "A white warrior must seek his own way." A long time ago, on another mission, Starfoot had fallen into the hands of men who had interrogated him with the help of injections of liquid sulphur. Billy Two had his lucid moments, but invariably on an assignment, as the mercs came closer to the ultimate battle, he came slightly unhinged. To the Indian, Hawk Spirit was the native equivalent of a guardian angel.

Dr. Hatton privately suspected that, under torture, Starfoot's psyche had snapped. When tension mounted and the mercs were repeatedly placed in life-and-death situations, imagining Hawk Spirit was with him was the only way the Osage had to deal with a major, chemically induced personality split. Billy Two became a six-and-a-half-foot, barrel-chested kid with an invisible friend.

No one could deny though that, on several occasions, Billy Two had pulled a couple of miracles from his sacred medicine pouch—thanks to Hawk Spirit, the Osage claimed. As a doctor, Lee Hatton would believe it when there was scientific proof.

Nile Barrabas didn't need proof. Billy Two was weird, but a hell of a warrior. He was someone to rely on when fighting got hot and the battle dicey. On a team of mercenaries, that was good enough.

Lee sauntered barefoot over to the bank of computers and leaned over Nate's shoulder to watch him work. "Now if we could just ask your computers where the bastards will strike, we could finish them off and get this thing over with."

"Actually Jessup and I have been trying that, Lee," Nate said earnestly. "We're using some standard game theory."

"That's what they use to figure out nuclear war scenarios, isn't it?"

"Exactly. But at a more basic level it's just a way of trying to anticipate your opponent's next move based on the assumption that he'll make an optimum choice."

"What do you mean?"

"Well, it's like two men who are arrested for a crime and taken into separate rooms for interrogation. Both men know that they'll probably get life. But the cops want an iron-clad case, so they tell each man that if he confesses and implicates the other, he'll get away with only seven years in jail. Imagine yourself alone in an interrogation room...."

"Who needs to imagine, Nate?" Starfoot growled from the other side of the room. "I've been there."

"Right, Billy Two. Well, in that situation, you have to figure out what the guy in the other interrogation room is doing. Using game theory, you can arrive at a series of probabilities of what his course of action will be. In the example I've just given, probably the other guy is going to talk. Since you'll end up getting life imprisonment, it's in your interest to talk first.''

"And be a stool for the rest of my life? I'd rather go to prison, Nate,'' Lee commented. "How does this help us right now?''

"Jessup and I have been feeding every imaginable scenario into the computer. Using some fairly complicated algebra, we've managed to calculate the likelihood of various actions that a group of terrorists on the loose in Florida might take. What we've been left with is a series of probabilities.''

"Not certainties?''

"Lee, there's only one certainty in life—that you'll bite the big one and bust through the pearly gates.''

"So what are you suggesting they're probably going to—''

The front door of the penthouse headquarters slammed. A bulky man in a soiled white suit chugged into the communications room. Huffing and puffing from the strain of moving his considerably over-weight body, Walker "The Fixer'' Jessup mopped beads of sweat from his plump red face with a handkerchief and swung a heavy black briefcase onto a table.

"I've got it, Nate,'' the burly Texan said, visibly excited and apparently oblivious to the presence of the other mercs. "Everything I could.'' He pressed the gold clasps and flung the case open, twisting it upside down. Hundreds of shiny tourist brochures slid into a pile on the table and spilled onto the floor.

"What in hell are these?" Hatton asked, grabbing some of the pamphlets as they fell and turning them over to read the printing. "Sea World? The Cypress Gardens?"

"Oh, hello, Lee," Jessup said distractedly, pawing through the brightly colored pamphlets. "Look! There are hundreds of them! Hundreds! Filled with thousands of people!" His voice wavered almost on the edge of hysteria. "Millions!" he cried, taking a big handful of the brochures and tossing them into the air.

His knees buckled underneath him and his bulky frame dropped heavily into a chair, which sagged almost to the point of collapse under his weight. His wide face cast the redness that his exertion had produced. Jessup turned white. He stared from Lee to Nate, afraid to utter another word. Hatton looked at Nate Beck.

"Does this have anything to do with that game theory you were telling me about?"

Beck swallowed, picking up a handful of the brochures and flipping through them. He nodded.

"We were called in after the raid on the plant in Pinellas and the hijacking on the interstate. As a result of the information we've been given, we've concentrated on military, defence industry and other vital targets. The authorities have encouraged us to think in that direction. But according to this—" Nate gave the top of the computer console a friendly whack with the palm of his hand, "—the chances of any of them being attacked are fairly minimal. And chances of a successful attack are even less, considering the beefed-up security systems."

"That means that Liam O'Toole and Claude Hayes are out on a wild goose chase right now," Lee concluded.

Nate shook his head. "Not necessarily. I'm hoping they'll uncover something. We still have no idea how many of these terrorists are here. The drop-off capacity of the deserted landing craft was more than fifty. For all we know, they were a ruse, and there are only ten or twenty terrorists here. Or the submersibles may have been filled to capacity and many more terrorists might have entered through other ports—air, land or sea. The point is that after we ran the program, the probabilities it gave us changed insignificantly in response to the number of potential attackers."

"But what does it mean, Nate?" Suddenly interested in their conversation, Billy Two loomed up behind the mercs seated at the computers.

In his rational moments, the Osage had a healthy skepticism for the electronic minds of the computer age. Their limitation was the reverse side of their strength. They operated on logic. Human beings didn't. That was why computers were forced to work with ranges and probabilities. But strange things happened in war, and if a warrior wasn't prepared for a bolt from the blue, he wasn't prepared period. That was where Hawk Spirit came in handy.

Nate cleared his throat. "Simply put, Billy, we asked the computers what a band of armed terrorists were likely to do in Florida besides work on their tans. Every time we ran the program, we came up with differing degrees of probability, even using the most extreme ranges of the existing variables, but the degree was always high and always for the same answer."

"The tourists," Jessup said flatly, looking at Hatton and Starfoot.

"The tourists," Nate confirmed, nodding. "That's the seminal fact about Florida, the one thing that makes it different from every other state at this time of year."

"It's spring break, the height of the season." Jessup said picking up on the explanation. "During the next three weeks, millions of people from the northern United States and Canada will pour into Florida. Families traveling to see Disney World, college kids off to Daytona Beach, jet setters heading for Coconut Grove, retired people descending on the Gulf beaches. Millions of them."

Nate Beck glanced up from his computer console and saw the approaching lights of an airborne vehicle. "That's the colonel's helicopter coming in now. He should be landing on the roof in about three and half minutes."

"It's about time," Lee sighed. "This waiting is enough to drive me crazy." She reached for her boots and began to pull them on again. "I'm going onto the roof to give the colonel a welcoming party."

Nate glanced quickly at his watch. Lee watched his face cloud over just as he swiveled around to check his computer monitor.

"What's happening, Nate?"

"Just checking if any data's come in."

Hatton finished lacing her boot up. "Geoff and Alex are overdue, aren't they?"

Beck swung around and faced her. "Only five minutes."

The woman looked at him, slightly grim. "Only? Come on, Nate. There's no such thing as 'only' in our business." She stood and walked toward the rooftop landing pad, leaving the three men to sit wordlessly inside.

Fanned by the warm breezes of fresh air blowing in from Tampa Bay, she watched the helicopter float in over MacDill and descend toward the landing pad on the roof. A fist of lead sat in the pit of her stomach, and she breathed with short, tight breaths, fighting anxiety. The chopper hovered several feet above the tarmac long enough for Barrabas to jump from the cabin door. Immediately the aircraft veered up to return to MacDill for refueling.

Barrabas held his MAC-10 tightly against his side as he ran toward Hatton and the doors of the penthouse.

"What's happening?" she shouted over the fading noise of the chopper's engines.

"We got it!" he yelled back, slapping Hatton's outstretched hand with his own in greeting. "They found submersibles exactly where we told them they'd be, and the governor was impressed. We have priority over the other law enforcement agencies to do this our way."

"Does that mean we take the yacht?"

"Damn right it does. Any word from the others?"

"Nothing from O'Toole and Hayes. Colonel, Geoff and Alex were due to report five minutes ago. They didn't."

The two mercs went inside.

"What's the word from Nanos and Bishop, Nate?" Barrabas shouted as he came into the main room of the SOBs' headquarters.

Beck remained at a console, his fingers flying along the keys. Occasionally he paused to examine the screen.

"They're not answering, Colonel. They're ignoring our signal completely. Or they're not picking it up."

"Contact the central operations post at MacDill and tell them to get a helicopter back up here on the double. Billy, Lee, get ready. We're going to pull out."

Barrabas tossed his MAC-10 into a chair and tugged his black sweatshirt over his head. He used it to wipe the sweat off his face and threw it beside the gun. Stripped down to a T-shirt, he stretched his neck and shoulders to ease the tightness. There was a muscle in his neck as rigid as a steel collar. He pulled against it, grunting as the knot eased its way out. Somewhere in the suite there was a Jacuzzi, graciously installed by an appreciative construction company after winning a generous contract from the general. Suddenly the Jacuzzi seemed like a good idea. Too bad there wasn't time.

Barrabas paced toward the large map of Florida on the wall, deep in thought. The red circles marking vital defence installations dotted the coastline and central region of the state. At Miami, Tampa Bay, Orlando and Cape Canaveral, they merged into huge clusters from the sheer density of the establishments.

"Forget all this," he told the others. "The enemy has different prey in mind. Terrorists crave sensational publicity for their causes. And dead bodies for their blood lust. The suicide massacres at airports in Tel Aviv, Vienna and Rome are the models we're looking at here. Pack a group of fanatics hell-bent on death in a crowded place with a few submachine guns and grenades, and the body count will be in the hundreds. I'll give anyone ten to one that when these bastards hit, it'll be among innocent people."

Walker Jessup picked up a handful of the Florida tourist pamphlets and looked at Lee. "And we needed four hundred thousand dollars worth of computers to tell us that? Don't tell Nate."

"There are hundreds of them," said Hatton. "Hundreds of tourist places where terrorists could strike. Why haven't these been considered? Why do the authorities keep harping about the danger to vital American defence interests?"

"Bah!" Billy Two exclaimed suddenly, his mouth set in a grimace of distaste. "Military is only interested in military. They don't want us to know."

"Oversight?" Jessup banged his plump fist on the arm of the chair. "Everyone's so damned afraid of terrorists getting hold of a nuclear device that they forgot about everything else at stake. A damned monster of an oversight."

"Walker, I've never heard you make such a bad call in the time I've known you, and that's since Nam," Barrabas said. "The reason we weren't briefed on the danger to tourists is probably because someone wanted our energy diverted in another direction."

"Deliberately?" Hatton asked shrewdly.

The colonel gave her an open-handed shrug. "Those terrorists in the house at Winter Park had been tipped in time to move out their main force. Draw your own conclusions.''

"Then it's a good thing they don't know about O'Toole and Hayes or what Geoff Bishop and Alex Nanos are up to.''

"That depends how high up the leaky mouth is," the colonel said softly.

He thought about the meeting at the mysterious compound at the edge of the Florida Everglades. In his mind's eye, he went around the table, examining each of the men who had been present. They were the only ones who had known about the yacht. Nanos and Bishop were now missing. He slipped his hand into a pocket and drew out the small numbered stub he had found in the villa in Winter Park. He handed it to Jessup. "Can you trace this?"

The Texan examined the small yellow ticket. "What is it?"

"That's what I want to know."

Beck turned from the telephone. "They're sending a chopper up here right away with a fresh pilot."

Barrabas turned to Lee Hatton and Billy Two. "Load up with ammo. Let's move it. Fast."

6

Liam O'Toole settled back to the roar of the diesel engine and the rhythm of the road as the giant Mack truck pulled its load down I-95. He glanced at Claude Hayes, who shared the cab with him. Taillights from the line of cars ahead of them left an undulating red glow across the black man's ebony face. The height of their seats gave both men almost a bird's-eye view of the night traffic streaming toward the delights of Florida beaches at spring break.

When Barrabas decided to put two of his men in to drive the arms shipment from South Carolina to West Palm Beach, Liam O'Toole was the natural choice as driver. The former army sergeant and demolitions and weapons expert was the only merc who knew how to throw together the right combination of gears and hydraulics to keep the heavy load on the road.

Claude Hayes had been in the U.S. Navy and fought as a freedom fighter in several African wars of independence. His talents included scuba and underwater warfare and demolitions. Like O'Toole, Claude Hayes was a big man, six feet of solid strapping muscle. They made a good pair in the world of truck drivers, and Claude knew enough about diesel rigs to act as backup.

"Going south," Claude boomed over the tinny sound of country music on the radio. "Look at them license plates—Michigan, Wisconsin, New York, Pennsylvania, Quebec. It's like an evacuation of the entire northeast. Course, one winter spent in a southern climate should be enough to persuade any man or woman of the folly of northern life."

"I thought you were from Detroit?"

"I am. But I lived in Africa, where it's always warm."

"Well, I'll tell you Claude, sitting up here, driving this rig down the interstate with a little lass singing country on the ra-di-ooo—" O'Toole crowed the word with a big smile, stretching the accents of his native Ireland as best he could to imitate a deep southern drawl "—it's pure Americana," he said. "Like a Burt Reynolds movie."

The Irishman leaned toward Hayes and lowered his voice, as if he were speaking confidentially. "My love for my adopted country surpasses my love of women—and you know how much I love the lady folk."

The taciturn Afro-American smiled slowly. "Yeah, I know what you mean," he said, nodding. "The country I almost left forever."

"Why, Claude?"

"In downtown Detroit there's an area called Watts, Liam. Last time I saw that place, it was just black smoke rising into a blue sky from all the burning buildings, and I was running from a riot and a policeman. You gotta grow up black in America to understand my reasons."

"Don't forget, Claude, I grew up Catholic in Belfast."

"Yeah, Liam. But you're still white. And living in this country that means you have a lot of privileges my people don't get. Even down here in Florida. We can drive into any one of these famous cities along the coast, and you're in a squeaky clean white world. The only time you'll see a black man is when he comes on Monday and Thursday to empty your garbage can. But they're there, a million or more of 'em, living in the poorer neighborhoods at the edge of the white cities or off in the country in tarpaper shacks on the side roads. There's real squalor down here, reserved for the black man and kept out of sight so the tourists don't know. I don't mean to put your experience down, Liam. I know Belfast was tough. But there ain't no experience like growing up black in America. Sometimes they don't just put you down—they make you invisible. And I didn't know that until I lived among my brothers in Africa. They don't know black pride over there, because they don't know black shame. They just live with the natural dignity that is a born right of every human being."

"So why'd you come back?"

Hayes rode for a few moments in silence. "Well, I suppose America's its own best advertisement. It's still a free country, and there are fewer and fewer of those in Africa these days. I did my time there, fighting in a few liberation movements, and I don't regret it. But I found out I'm an American first. I didn't belong there. Everyone in Africa belonged to a tribe, and when they asked me what tribe I belonged to, I'd say, no tribe. And they all thought that was pretty strange. And you know what else? One day I thought about all those young black kids at home, growing up and feeling bad about being black. I suppose I figured I could be a role model."

"You, a role model?" O'Toole looked at Hayes with mock horror. "Don't tell the mommas and lock up the dottas!"

"Hot damn," Claude Hayes chuckled at his friend's joke.

O'Toole suddenly sat up straight and slammed his foot on the brakes. A big silver 68 Cadillac with New Jersey plates had pulled into the passing lane, changed its mind and returned to the right side of the highway a few inches from the front bumper of the Mack truck. The hydraulics sighed, the tires screeched and the deceleration threw the two men forward. Then the driver of the Caddy reduced his speed to a range roughly adequate for a school zone in a pedestrian mall.

"Goddamn tourists!" O'Toole roared. There was just enough space in the passing lane between the red taillights in front and a pair of headlights rapidly approaching from the rear. His hands flew, downshifting, flicking the turn signal on, rolling the steering wheel to the left and shifting up.

"Don't forget we got two military intelligence agents on our tail that we ain't supposed to lose," Claude Hayes reminded the hotheaded driver.

"They ought to build a truck to chew up bad drivers and fart them out as exhaust. Roll down your window there and tell the guy to get a tricycle."

Hayes looked down as the heavy truck drew alongside the silver Cadillac. A white-haired man of advanced age clutched the steering wheel and peered through the windshield, the tip of his nose two inches from the glass. A least half the cars they'd passed since Jacksonville had had that kind of driver. They were one of the two hazards of highway driving in Florida.

"Liam, that guy hasn't ridden a tricycle in sixty years."

As if on cue, the second major hazard of the highways flashed into view. A red Trans Am, with a row of spoilers running down the rear window like scales on a lizard, zipped up behind the silver Caddy and practically kissed its chrome bumper.

There were two kinds of dangerous gators in the state of Florida: alligators and tailgaters. Claude Hayes preferred the former. They killed to eat. The second kind killed because they had some kind of macho notion of how to drive.

The Mack's diesel engines roared. Tractor and trailer surged past the silver Cadillac, and O'Toole pulled back into the right lane. Immediately the red Trans Am flashed by them, tearing up the highway until the driver was forced to brake abruptly when he reached the next car that was driving at a normal speed.

"Rest stop in twelve miles," Hayes said, glancing at his watch. "And we're on time."

Their itinerary had been carefully prepared well in advance, allowing their escort to drive at a safe and unobservable distance on the busy highway. There were also prearranged catch-up points at truck stops along the interstate. The citizen's band radio under the dash wasn't to be used unless absolutely necessary.

"Have you seen our escort lately?"

"Not for a while."

"I'm going to get that guy in the Trans Am. He's a goddamned highway maniac," O'Toole muttered, narrowing his eyes as he pressed the accelerator. The heavy truck surged forward, and he pulled into the passing lane again.

"What do you mean?" Hayes asked, a little unsure of his buddy's actions.

"I mean we got twelve miles before we pull off the highway for a coffee. I'm going to burn that guy's smart ass because he's burning mine."

Ten tons of mighty steel rolled on a straightaway down the passing lane, hurtling by the line of cars, trailers and RVs snaking along the interstate. O'Toole flicked his high beams on and off as the Mack truck came up behind cars in the passing lane. No one argued. They got out of his way.

"Perfect," O'Toole muttered, forcing his total concentration on the road and the gears. The red Trans Am was straight in front of him. And after that was a solid knot of cars in both lanes that stretched almost half a mile up the road.

Maintaining a steady spead, he pushed the truck forward, flicking his high beams on and off as he approached the Trans Am's taillights. The driver of the souped-up sports car ignored O'Toole and pushed at the tail end of a tiny little Honda in front. The Honda moved. O'Toole flicked his high beams again, squeezing the accelerator. The truck bore down on the taillights of the Trans Am. The driver still refused to move. Facing imminent collision, the red-haired Irishman hit the horn.

The ear-splitting blasts from each side of the hood were as persuasive as the fancy chrome grille driving into the Trans Am's rearview mirror. The sports car moved fast, lurching into the right lane as the diesel slammed past.

O'Toole checked out the rearview mirror. Traffic was already moving in behind him to fill the space. He took his foot off the gas pedal and eased the truck back into the right lane, in front of the Trans Am. Cars and RVs pulled past him on the left, then slowed as they came up behind the knot of traffic that clogged the highway ahead.

"Man, you are one mother of a driver," Hayes told him, half laughing. "I don't know who's more dangerous, you or the cat in that fancy fire engine behind us."

"I'm not half-finished yet." Wedged in solidly by the truck in front and the traffic behind and to the side, the Trans Am was pulling up fast, this time on O'Toole's tail.

The Irishman slowed, forcing the red car to brake. Then he evened out his speed. The Trans Am pulled up tight and hung on, with barely inches left between the bumper of the trailer and the front of the sports car.

O'Toole tapped the brakes just a little.

The rig jerked and slowed. A grinding noise and an additional vibration rocked through the cab of the truck. In the side mirror, O'Toole saw a shower of sparks fly as the front of the Trans Am almost ignited against his steel rear bumper. His foot flew to the gas pedal at the bare second of collision. Once again the truck sped forward, leaving the Trans Am eating the truck's wind and honking wildly.

"Gotcha!" O'Toole shouted.

Hayes shook his head, disapprovingly. "Man, you're trying to make a point and you end up as bad as he is."

"You think so?" O'Toole sounded doubtful.

"Yeah, man. I'm sure so."

"I'll tell you, Claude, it isn't every day you get to use a diesel rig to throw your weight at a jerk driver. Oh, oh. Here he comes again, looking for more."

There was a break in the traffic. Suddenly the Trans Am shot around the rear end of the truck and scooted alongside. The driver evened out his speed to parallel the rig.

"Well, don't give it to him," Hayes admonished. "A driver like that will always come back for more until one or both of you gets . . ."

"Shit! Get back! Oh Christ!" O'Toole looked up from the side window, the whites of his eyes suddenly prominent in his freckled face. "He's waving a bloody gun!"

The Irishman hit the brakes. Once again tires screeched, hydraulics sighed, and the two men bounced out of their seats toward the windshield. The Trans Am tore past them, and a hand holding a gun disappeared inside the passenger's window.

"Crazy fucker," O'Toole cursed in relief.

"You or him? Someone should've told you about handgun laws in this state. There aren't none, and rule number one is don't get into unnecessary arguments, Liam, cause down here, you never know who's packing what. And they's all looking for excuses."

"I'll remember that, buddy. For next time. Say, when's the oasis?"

"Six miles."

"Great. I can use the breather."

The highway rest stop appeared, an explosion of neon in the country night. A herd of diesel rigs studded with running lights, slumbered like beasts on a veldt of asphalt. The fueling area was bathed in white fluorescence. The air hummed with electricity. Underneath the flashing light bulbs that spelled out Eat, the soft glow in the windows of a ranch-style restaurant looked cozy and inviting.

O'Toole and Hayes stepped down from the cab. Their truck was sandwiched between two rigs of similar size and faced the service area. The air was tangy with diesel fumes from the gas pumps and exhausts. The sounds of cars speeding past on the nearby highway was all but drowned out by the sonorous chugging of diesel engines.

A few truckers lolled about outside the cabs of their rigs. Attendants in white coveralls jumped to pump gas, wash windows and check oil. Tourists—the elderly in flashy Lincolns and Eldorados, the students in sleek Fieros and economical Datsuns—parked and wandered to the restaurant. Their numbers had dwindled to fewer than a dozen with the lateness of the hour.

"I'll check it out, Liam, if you want," Hayes offered. "Get some coffee, see if our buddies from military intelligence are around, relieve myself and come back to relieve you. Still take yours black?"

"Lighten it up this time." O'Toole stood under the open door, trying to spot the dark Oldsmobile that carried their tails. "Hey, listen. You were right back there on the highway."

"Forget it."

"No, really. Especially with the kind of load we're traveling with. It's the red hair. Hothead, get it? " O'Toole stuck his index finger into his temple and turned it. "Stupid."

"Hey, few people know how boring our line of work really is. You gotta spice it up somehow." Hayes gave O'Toole a friendly pat on the shoulder.

The Irishman's voice suddenly softened as the black merc turned to go. "Claude, think anyone's going to take the bait?"

"I dunno, Liam," Hayes said, stopping momentarily. He patted the left side of his jacket where he could feel the reassuring hardness of his pistol. "I got mine. You got yours?"

"I got mine," O'Toole confirmed. "But I'll wait up in the cab close to the shotgun and the MAC-10."

"See you in a minute." Hayes started across the vast parking area.

The restaurant was a long low bungalow faced with fake log siding. A polished pine plank hung above the door with the name Trading Post and Chow House burned into it. There were blue gingham curtains in the windows and hanging kerosene lamps with electric light bulbs in them. Just before he reached the door he saw the gleaming black Olds parked off to the side. Their tail had preceded them. He reminded himself not to look for them, not even to acknowledge them inside. Just as he opened the bug-splattered screen door, he noticed that a red Trans Am had pulled in, too.

"Hey, there! How ya doing tonight? Is everything all right?" asked a bright-eyed blond woman in a pink pantsuit and a little white apron as she went by, a steaming Pyrex coffeepot poised in one hand. Her greeting was genuinely friendly and definitely southern in its dips and drawls. In the south, friendliness assaulted a man. Southerners were proud of their hospitality.

"I'm fine, thank you, ma'am. Just drove in from Jacksonville," Claude said, remembering to give like for like.

"You're a trucker then? Truckers have that side of the restaurant, and we got a special for you on steak and eggs, mister." She pointed to Claude's right. A dozen or so burly men sat in small groups, their thick forearms resting on the tables, which held steaming cups and plates piled high with food. A few looked casually toward the door out of curiosity and turned back to their friends when they failed to recognize Hayes.

"Just a couple of coffees to go," Claude told the waitress. "And the use of your facilities." He moved slightly to his left to look into the dining room, where a smattering of tourists and other travelers were eating, their tones hushed. There was no sign of the agents. The understanding was that they would find a table near the door, which shouldn't have been difficult in the nearly empty restaurant.

"Why sure, you just sit at the counter over there and George'll get it for you. George! George!" she crowed across the restaurant until she had the attention of a hefty man with stringy grey hair who was working the grill behind the counter. "Two coffees to go for this gentleman!"

George gave a solemn nod and wiped his hands on his stained apron. He reached for the quart-sized Styrofoam cups and a pot of thick-looking coffee. Hayes swung his leg over a stool and leaned on the counter as the cook set the cups in front of him. A big burly trucker with a beer gut oozing out from under his shirt was wolfing down a plate of steak and eggs three stools down. The black soldier was aware of a few heads turning, and he knew the kind of stares he was getting. The big guy seemed particularly disturbed and turned to confer with his two buddies who sat beside him.

"Regular?" George dead panned, looking Claude in the eyes, "Or black?"

"A little whitener. And some lids if you got 'em."

The short order cook broke out in a grin and winked at Hayes."Cream's right down there," he said, pointing to a stainless steel pitcher down the counter. "And lids are coming right up, mister." He moved away and reached under the counter.

Feeling the stares from the direction of the trucker with the beer gut, Hayes turned to face him. The man looked mean, ugly and stupid enough to pick a fight.

"Can you hand me the cream, please?" Hayes pointed to the little pitcher.

For a moment, the trucker didn't move. Then he picked up the pitcher and emptied the cream into his own coffee. After shaking the last few drops out, he looked inside and turned to Hayes.

"Wa-lll, I'll be damned if it ain't empty!" he said, feigning surprise. A thin toothy smile creased his mug, and his immense belly jiggled with chuckles. His two friends laughed at the enormously funny joke.

Hayes tightened. The moment of choice was familiar—to fight or, for the time being, to retreat. Wait to see if the tough guy was bluffing like a rooster puffing up his chest for the benefit of all the chickens in the hen house, or if he was serious enough to cause real trouble. Claude Hayes knew the moment. He'd been there before.

George's hefty arm swept across the counter, depositing a full pitcher of cream in front of Hayes.

"Never mind," he sighed calmly. "Never you mind, mister. You're always welcome at the Chow House." Suddenly he lifted his head and shouted. "Mabel!"

The waitress emerged from the other dining room, her pen poised above her order pad.

"Mabel, these gentlemen here—" the short order cook pointed to the three pranksters at the counter. "—they want their check. Don't you, boys?"

"Forget it!" Hayes stood and, holding the coffee, backed away from the counter. The man with the gut stood, a sneer curling up the side of his face. His two friends looked on with silly smiles.

"Tom Strathers, are you making trouble out here again!" Mabel marched toward the three men, her arms waving furiously. "Dick Coughlin, is that you sitting there? And Harry Rimmer, what are you doing out here with your wife at home with a new baby?"

The big man suddenly looked a lot smaller, and the others quickly turned back to their coffees, hunching their shoulders over the counter. Mabel turned to Hayes with an apologetic look. "Mister, you don't pay no mind to these boys. They just forgot their manners. You come back now, y'hear."

"Thank you, ma'am. I surely will." Hayes tipped his head at the short-order cook and headed toward the men's room on his way out. As he passed the main dining room, he searched, again in vain, for a sign of the backup men from military intelligence.

Perplexed and somewhat worried, he pushed through the rest room door.

There was a row of sinks, a row of urinals, a row of hand dryers and four cubicles. The ceiling was a single, giant fluorescent light. The strong odor of antiseptic assaulted his nostrils. A low steady hum indicated a ventilation fan somewhere.

Hayes set the coffee on one of the stainless steel shelves over a sink and pushed against a cubicle door. Locked, apparently occupied. The one beside it was occupied as well. He chose the last one, went inside and closed the door behind him. Something was bothering him deeply, gnawing at him from the inside. He stopped a moment, trying to think. It was the occupied cubicles. When he came into the rest room, no feet had been visible under the doors.

Hayes got down on his hands and knees and looked under the metal partition. He was right. The cubicles were empty, apparently locked from the inside. He stood up and went outside,trying the doors once again. Both were firmly locked. He went up close, and looked over the top.

Whoever had done it, had done it well.

The bodies of both agents had been turned upside down, their legs propped against the walls and their heads lowered into the toilets. Their throats had been neatly slit from ear to ear, and the toilet bowls were filled with pools of deep red blood.

Hayes gagged, the contents of his stomach forcing its way upward. He made it to the sink and puked, the horrible image of the dead men burned into his retina.

O'Toole. The truck. The terrorists had taken the bait. They were there now. Claude Hayes spat, wiped his sleeve across his mouth and rushed from the rest room.

7

Like razor blades cutting black silk, the dorsal fins of the sharks silently slit the surface of the water. The hungry predators made a wide arc through the line of the yacht's spotlight and slipped into the inky darkness beyond.

They were circling.

Geoff Bishop felt panic rising from his gut as the giant carnivorous fish disappeared. His legs and body were chillingly vulnerable beneath the surface of the water. He could not know when they would come or from what direction. But come they would. The panic rose, becoming a scream paralysed in his throat.

He clutched Nanos tightly around the chest and kicked hard, stretching his free arm in the direction of the light. The exertion steadied his terror. He glanced to each side as he swam, straining his eyes against the night for a sign of the dreadful beasts. Bits of wreckage from the Italian cruiser floated past him, thin sheets of fiberglass and splintered paneling, nothing large enough to serve as a flotation device. At least, Alex Nanos offered no resistance. The unconscious man bobbed gently in the waves as Bishop pulled him in a chest carry.

The yacht appeared to be moving away from them. The blinding yellow spot grew smaller across the water. As Bishop reached forward, his arm struck something smooth and cold. A shudder rippled through him, and his heart pounded from fear of the sharks that lurked in the mysterious depths nearby. He turned to look at the hard, smooth object.

It was the cooler from the cockpit of the boat, sealed tight and floating half out of the water. Bishop grabbed for it. His hand clutched the tiny steel clasp at the center just as a wave pushed between him and the cooler. Feverishly, he hooked his thumb into the catch and flicked it open. Then the wave tore his hand away.

He kicked and pulled forward, looking quickly to ensure that Nanos's head remained above water. He reached out again, this time forcing the lid of the cooler open and grabbing the inside rim as the lid slammed back down. With another kick and a forceful push with the back of his arm, he flipped the lid all the way open and held on tightly.

The plastic-covered, Styrofoam-insulated box was almost as long as a bathtub. Geoff Bishop was damned sure it could float two people. He looked down at the unconscious man in his arms.

"Hey, buddy," he whispered, aware of the strenuous feat that lay ahead. His energy level had ebbed, but he demanded more, drawing the last reserves of strength from his body. "Help me out on this, buddy, just this once."

The airman loosened his grip on the unconscious merc's chest and grabbed one of his arms. He pushed it over the rim of the cooler, and held it there. Then he brought Nanos's other arm up, crossed it over the first one at the wrist and pinned them together with his hand. The Greek's head dropped back, his face well away from the waves. The trick now was for Bishop to get into the giant cooler without filling it with water. If one side went even a fraction of an inch too low, the waves would pour in and it would be game over. There was a way. He had learned it as a kid during one of his summers on a cold lake in the northern Canadian woods. His father had shown him how to get into a canoe from the water.

The critical factor was weight distribution. Holding Nanos's arms securely against the rim of the cooler, Bishop moved to one end of it. The lid already pulled on one side, balancing Nanos's drag. The airman cautiously put his other arm on the box and flutter kicked to push himself forward. The box tipped, giving him better access. He threw his weight into his arms and head, kicked hard and flung his upper torso forward.

The cooler dipped as Geoff Bishop fell on his face in the bottom, still clutching Alex Nanos. He twisted onto his back and sat up. The cooler floated almost a foot deeper in the water, but there was still more than a foot yet to go. Quickly he moved to the side and pulled Nanos up. When he had the merc's limp body halfway into the cooler, he dragged Nanos's legs over sideways. Then he collapsed against his unconscious companion, exhausted.

After a moment, squeezing out from under the Greek, Bishop tried to sit up. A wave hit the cooler as he moved, splashing over the edge. He froze, checking the weight distribution. Slowly he adjusted his position, evening out the line of the cooler, as it rocked in the waves. Something had changed. The night pushed in around him like a smothering cloth pressed over his face. Nothing was visible. The yacht was gone. Bishop was mystified by its rapid disappearance and wondered if he had passed out for an unknown length of time. It was impossible for the yacht to have disappeared that quickly.

He could barely make out Alex Nanos's face in the darkness. His touch told him that the ugly wound in the merc's chest had almost stopped bleeding. Bishop stripped off his drenched shirt and ripped it, folding part of it into a square, which he pressed into the gaping hole in Alex's flesh.

Something scraped along the underside of the cooler.

A terrible chill rippled up his spine. He gripped the edge of the box tightly as panic's cold hand tightened on his neck. He recognized again the eerie, almost supernatural terror the shark created in him, and he fought it, his hands trembling as he tore the rest of his shirt into long strips.

An object thudded against the side of the cooler, jolting it. Almost in front of his eyes, a jet-black triangle cut the water near the cooler and disappeared again into the unknown world beneath the waves.

"O, sweet Lord," Geoff Bishop prayed, rapidly tying a bandage around Alex's shoulder and binding the wound. The merc's pulse had strengthened and was regular. Nanos might live. If they survived the sharks.In front of Bishop, the waters parted and the long shiny body of the giant fish slammed against the bathtub-sized cooler, tilting it. The weight of the lid pulled it back, but water had already swept in at one of the corners. The cooler sank lower in the water as the shark disappeared beneath the waves.

The Canadian was suddenly aware of the muffled throbbing of powerful inboard engines. He jerked his head quickly around.

"My god," he gasped, less in prayer than in amazement.

The bow of the hundred-foot yacht, its lights extinguished, bore down on the two men in the tiny makeshift lifeboat, cleaving the waves like the great dark blade of a giant axe.

LIAM O'TOOLE TURNED OFF THE RADIO and surveyed the highway oasis from high in the cab of the truck. He hummed a small Irish ditty for a minute and realized that the last two hundred miles of driving had sapped his energy. The truck stop was on the outskirts of Melbourne, just south of Cape Canaveral and the Kennedy Space Center. They had another hundred miles to go to West Palm Beach. Maybe Hayes could drive for the next hour or so while he grabbed a bit of shut-eye. There was a little bunk up behind the seats of the cab. Assuming they didn't run into trouble before then, of course.

Speculating that the terrorists might try to hijack the truckload of arms and missiles was a shot in the dark—a pretty good one, considering how little they had to go on. But so far, sailing down the highway in the diesel rig had been smooth, and the weather looked good for the rest of the drive. Liam O'Toole had no nasty premonitions of impending danger.

He heard footsteps and a cough outside the truck and waited for Claude Hayes to pull up to the door and hand him his coffee. A few moments later his fellow merc still hadn't shown and the footsteps had gone away. He glanced out the window. The area around the truck was deserted.

"Claude?" he called. No answer.

He opened the door and stepped onto the first rung of the short metal ladder.

"Claude?"

Silence. He reached inside his jacket and slipped his Walther P-38 from its holster. Slowly he stepped down, straining for the slightest noise.

The back of his head exploded into his eyeballs, the neon signs of the highway oasis dancing and disintegrating into colored pinpricks before his eyes. He felt monstrous pain and warm blood course down the back of his neck. His body collapsed despite the strenuous effort of his will.

His knees hit the ground as he struggled to regain his vision. Two men were standing in front of him and a third was climbing quickly up the ladder to the cab. The door on the other side of the truck slammed shut, and someone issued an order in a foreign language.The field of blackness before O'Toole's eyes began to clear. He pushed himself backward, rolling away from the men near the cab just in time to see Claude Hayes burst around the corner of the truck. O'Toole's pistol hung loosely inside his jacket. He tried to reach for it but collapsed under the weight of pain at the back of his head.

Hayes was there, taking hold of O'Toole under his shoulders and hoisting him to his feet. One of the attackers had boarded the truck and started the motor. Two more stood by the front wheels. One held a crowbar. The other a Magnum. With their backs to the harsh lights of the fueling area, their faces were masked by shadow. O'Toole used Claude to support his weight as he stood.

"Tirez. Tirez!" the man with the crowbar shouted in French to his friend with the Magnum, urging him to fire.

Hayes backed up rapidly, pulling O'Toole after him. He had his right arm around the Irishman's waist, concealing his gun against the folds of Liam's jacket.

"Non!" the terrorist answered. The hand that held the Magnum dropped.

The two mercs backed away as the diesel rig pulled forward from its parking space. When they reached the end of the neighboring truck, they ran.

The terrorist who held the gun laughed. "No," he said, smoothing his thick moustache. "By the time they raise the alarm, we will have taken what we want from the truck and be gone. We can spare the drivers. After all, they are workers."

The man with the crowbar looked at him strangely. "An odd sentiment," he said coolly, "considering who we will be killing tomorrow."

Claude Hayes helped Liam O'Toole lean against the bumper of a rig in another part of the huge parking area.

"You okay?"

O'Toole groaned and felt the back of his head. It was soft, and mushy and his hand came away bloody.

"Thanks, old buddy. Yeah, I'm all right. Why didn't they kill us?"

"I dunno," Hayes said slowly. "The two agents on our tail weren't as lucky. Look. There they go."

The two men watched the truck disappear down the ramp leading back to the highway.

"Whew," O'Toole sighed with relief. "The luck of the Irish comes through again. We got our lives."

"Yeah. And we better call Barrabas, cause we just got our first big break."

NATE BECK SAT with Walker Jessup in the empty command post as the helicopter carrying Barrabas, Hatton and Starfoot disappeared over Tampa Bay. The two men looked at each other.

"I don't know what to do," Jessup said finally, slapping his knees in a gesture of futility. Nate realized he was referring to the missing mercs.

"Nothing you can do, 'cept wait until we hear from the colonel." The computer wizard tinkered at the keyboard of one of his gadgets. His face was grim in the ghostly green and amber lights cast from the rows of monitors. Working as a team—often saving each other's lives—cemented the bonds of comradeship between the mercs. With Alex Nanos and Nate Beck, friendship had extended into their free time, as well. Almost inevitably the two men had spent time on grand binges—usually arranged by Alex Nanos—in between missions.

"Hey," he called to Jessup, "you remember the time you and the colonel found Alex and I wandering naked on the New Jersey Turnpike? It was after the mob threw us out of the hotel in Atlantic City."

The Fixer smiled and nodded. "Yeah, the Greek, he sure knows how to party, hot damn!"

The two men fell into an almost embarrassed silence, acutely aware of the unspoken fear they shared. All of them knew the risks, and it was an irony of their job that, despite the bonds of brotherhood, as professionals none of them could allow sentimentality to interfere with the job at hand.

Jessup held up the small numbered stub Barrabas had given him and scrutinized it. "Guess I better start tracking this down," he said softly.

A red light on a telephone console began to flash in accompaniment with a soft persistent beep. Nate grabbed it.

"Beck, here." He looked over his shoulder at Jessup, who watched, his eyes wide with expectation. "O'Toole!" he mouthed for the Texans' benefit. Jessup's eyes lit up. Beck cupped his hand over the mouthpiece. "They took the bait!"

Before he had finished the sentence, his hands were flying, tapping instructions into the computers and moving along the banks of electronic equipment, switching on tracking screens and monitors. The telephone conversation was terse and monosyllabic.

"Gotcha!" Beck concluded. "Stay tuned." He slammed the telephone receiver down and turned to Jessup. "The shipment was hijacked. Hayes and O'Toole are okay, but the two agents bought it. The boys are taking the agents' car and will start tracking as soon as I feed the information back out to them."

Jessup leaned over Beck's shoulder and stared at the cold green light of the main monitor. "This technology still amazes me, Nate. Makes me feel like I went to secret agent school back in the nineteenth century."

"It's simple, Walker. Not even sophisticated really. The trucks and the crates of arms inside were marked with radioactive isotopes implanted in the shipping material. It's not dangerous enough to harm people, but for the duration of its four-day half-life, it's strong enough to be tracked by one of our new civilian satellites, using infrared detection devices." He pointed to a cable as thick as a man's wrist that coiled along the floor before dividing into the terminals along the wall. "That leads to the dish on the roof. The satellite will pick up a lot of noise—radioactive samples in dentists' labs, college laboratories, there's even a smoke detector factory somewhere in Orange County as I recall, and they use small amounts of radioactive material—but the computers will clean out the static signals and any that don't conform to the isotope we're using. It'll show us the movement of the truck, or if the arms are off-loaded, their distribution. In a few moments, I'll start getting a readout on this monitor here." He patted a nine-inch screen on his left. "It'll look like a radar blimp. Underneath the image we'll get general information on how fast they're traveling and what direction they're going. But the main computer over there is the real brains behind the operation."

The words STAND BY appeared suddenly on the screen. Nate typed in some instructions. READY TO RECEIVE replaced the first message.

"Here we go." The computer beeped, and the screen sprang to life, displaying a giant circle swept by a single long clock hand. As it passed around the right side of the screen, a small green dot was illuminated, and the computer beeped again. Nate typed in further instructions. Data appeared at the bottom of the monitor.

"It's traveling north-northwest at seventy-two miles an hour. Now the real work is done over here."

Beck stood and walked quickly to a large color monitor perched above a console. He typed instructions quickly on the keyboard, and an outline of Florida appeared on the screen. Thin vertical and horizontal lines superimposed over the image formed a grid with mapping coordinates along the bottom and side.

"Wait'll you see this. It's incredible."

A small blinking dot appeared in a square halfway up Florida's east coast. Beck typed in the square's coordinates. The screen flashed, and the image was replaced by another one showing details of the intricate highway system along the coast. The color monitor clearly marked urban areas in yellow and the road systems in red and blue. The grid across the screen remained constant, and the flashing dot was positioned in the center of the screen moving along a thick red line,

"The truck is moving straight up I-95, just south of Cocoa Beach and the Kennedy Space Center. We can get closer." Once again Nate pressed a key. This time the image showed details of a highway interchange, surrounded by areas delineated in pink and green.

"The pink area is residential. Green marks countryside. The truck is passing the interchange right now and continuing north on I-95."

"The satellite shows all that?" Jessup asked, incredulous.

"Actually, no. The satellite only transmits to us extremely precise coordinates of the radioactive material it's tracking. The computer is programmed to fill in the rest by superimposing the maps of Florida over the satellite coordinates. As soon as that truck heads off the main highway, I can follow it down every street. If it stops, I can pinpoint its location within two or three buildings."

"How do O'Toole and Hayes get the information?"

"It's done already. Scrambled radio transmission. I just press a button. The computers are transmitting the data automatically to a digital read out in the agents' car. O'Toole and Hayes can follow and stay out of sight. The only limitation concerns the concentration of the arms. Once they're distributed from the crates to individual terrorists, the radioactive signals given off by the isotope will be too faint for the satellite to continue tracking."

"Which means we have to keep right on top of them so they won't have that chance," said Jessup.

"Which may not be the easiest thing in the world," Beck commented. He looked up at Jessup. "Considering we're spread a little thin right now."

The Fixer looked at the yellow ticket stub still clenched between his fingers. "Guess I'll give this little lead a go and see where it takes us. I got someone who owes me a favor in St. Pete. Criminal scientist. I hope he doesn't mind being woke up. How 'bout you?"

"Me? I sit here and follow a satellite following a truck." Nate Beck stood, pushing away from the computer and leaning over a radio transmitter. He flicked on a switch to activate a scrambler. "But first, I call the colonel."

"LET'S GO WITH THE SEARCHLIGHT," Barrabas ordered the helicopter pilot.

Landry Carter reached for a switch and suddenly a column of light beamed down from the chopper, illuminating the black water a hundred feet below. The light moved automatically back and forth across the surface of the ocean, a giant finger probing empty depths.

When Barrabas's requested helicopter had arrived on the rooftop landing pad, the Delta Force major had stuck his head out the cockpit window with a smile and a thumbs up.

"I really was with the 160 Airborne," he told Barrabas as the mercs jumped aboard. "My initial training was helicopters. I chicken-hawked three years in Nam. When I learned you were using pilots, I called in a few favors. Hope you don't mind."

Barrabas flashed a big smile of greeting at the clean-cut, green-eyed man. "So sometimes the old-boy network can be useful." He winked.

"No comment." Carter said, laughing as he raised the collective and adjusted the throttle to lift the chopper off the roof. He headed in the direction of the Gulf of Mexico, thirty miles away on the other side of Tampa Bay.

The chopper had flown to Bean Point, the northern tip of Anna Maria Key, using sophisticated tracking equipment to bring them over the Italian cruiser's last reported location. Constant attempts to contact Nanos and Bishop by scrambler and standard marine band radio during the flight had failed. The air waves were empty, and there were no visible lights from either boat. The two mercs, their boat and the yacht they were keeping under surveillance had disappeared under the blanket of night.

"Take it lower and skim over the surface," Barrabas instructed Carter. A quiet beep and a flashing red light alerted him. Someone was making radio contact. Nate Beck spoke from the Tampa base.

"Red Dog to Manatee, urgent. Are you reading? Over."

"Manatee reading, Red Dog. Over."

"The lure was good, Manatee, and the fish have taken the bait. Am tracking. Over."

"Directions, Red Dog. Over."

"Manatee, the subject is currently at rest, possibly for distribution and separation. Urgent need for backup. Computer probabilities suggest Daytona Beach and Orlando as possible destinations. Advise. Over."

"Positions, over."

"Fishermen suggest maintaining position northbound. Over."

As the helicopter descended, the circular beam of the search light grew wider across the surface, penetrating jade-green water to a depth of several feet. Flotsam and jetsam floated in the peaks and troughs of the roiling waves.

"Stand by, Red Dog." Barrabas moved the mouthpiece aside, and leaned out the window. Fiberglass debris. Bits of junk.

"Could be from anything," Carter said.

"Yup. Could be." Barrabas's quick agreement sounded doubtful.

"If the yacht moved out, they might have followed," Billy Two suggested, moving forward from the rear seat to speak.

Lee Hatton, sitting beside the Osage, shook her head. "They would have made contact. And where are their lights? How far could they have traveled in an hour?"

The colonel checked his watch. Two hours had elapsed since the mercs had last reported to Nate. The terrorists' yacht was a sleek new French design and, despite the length of its beam, could easily manage fifty miles an hour. If the two mercs were still on the yacht's tail, they could be a hundred miles away. In any direction. Thousands of square miles to cover. An hour yet to daylight. And the mercs had a job to do.

"That looks like the debris from a high-power, heavy-impact explosion down there. If you ask me, we should forget it." The team's doctor sank back heavily in her seat. Her eyes were resolute in acknowledgment of the terrible fact that Nanos and Bishop were missing, presumed dead.

Barrabas called the tough ones. That was his job, the job of commanding of a unit of military people whose paid profession was to put their lives on the line over and over again. This was the toughest call a military commander had to make. He had to face it; his soldiers depended on him. It was something called trust, and it was the only thing that made the group work as a team.

In the circumstances—the certainty that the terrorists were going to strike somewhere soon—there was only one decision he could make. If Bishop and Nanos were all right, there was no problem. If they were not all right, they were beyond help.

He turned around and looked Lee Hatton straight in the eyes.

"We got work to do," she said to him, meeting his stare straight on.

"It's an hour to dawn. I'll make sure the whole goddamned navy is out searching those waters."

"I know you will," said Lee.

"How long does it take to go to Orlando?" Barrabas asked the pilot from Delta Force.

"Half an hour. Maybe less. We go as the crow flies, and we can see Wonderworld on the way."

"And Daytona Beach or I-95, the Atlantic coast?"

"Half an hour again."

Barrabas spoke into the transmitter again.

"Manatee calling Red Dog. Are you still receiving? Over."

"Red Dog receiving Manatee loud and clear. Awaiting instructions. Over."

"Manatee proceeding to Orlando and points farther east. Keep us tuned in. Over and out."

Barrabas looked from the window as the chopper rose dramatically away from the water toward the northeast, his eyes searching among the floating debris for the last time.

There were pieces of white fiberglass from the hull of the boat and something that might have been part of the cockpit control panel. A big white cooler floated upside down, almost under the surface, its white enamel side reflecting the searchlight. Pieces of junk, lots of it, but no sign at all of two men in the roughening waves.

8

The truck drove off I-95 south of Titusville, near where the interstate was intersected by the Bee Line Expressway. Just past the interstate, the truck passed a vast roadside camp where a battered metal sign advertised the Sleep-A-Wee Trailer Park in a random combination of flickering and burned-out light bulbs. Hundreds of recreational vehicles, mobile homes and tent trailers had put in for the night, their slumbering owners oblivious to the nightmare raging outside their doors. The truck turned into a deserted picnic area two hundred yards farther on.

Hayes parked the black Oldsmobile off I-95, half a mile from the spot their tracking device indicated that the truck had turned off. The two men broke open the supply of arms and ammunition that the military agents had placed in the trunk. Hayes stayed with the car, informing Nate Beck of their current position for transmission to Barrabas and the other mercs.

Armed with a compact MAC-10 submachine gun, O'Toole covered the distance on foot, creeping through a bug-infested swamp to spy on the hijackers from the cover of the forest. Hungry mosquitoes buzzed happily against his bare head and arms as

O'Toole carefully pushed aside some branches to look into the clearing.

He was soaked with fetid water up to his knees, his face and arms stung from scratches inflicted by stubborn, subtropical vegetation, and the mosquitos already present were inviting their friends. Their wiry buzzing was like the sound of a high-speed drill, a sound that fit perfectly with what they were busy doing to his skin.

He dared not move.

Two cars came down the narrow road past the trailer camp—a Toyota and the red Trans Am. They parked beside the truck.

O'Toole thought of an old saying he had learned in his early days when he had strayed from the path and ran bombs for the IRA in his homeland. Once is happenstance, twice is coincidence, three times is enemy action. It was the third time in a matter of hours that his path had crossed that of the red sports car and its manic driver. This was a killing he might enjoy.

The cars and truck were at rest with their engines running and their parking lights on. Two men emerged from each vehicle. In the darkness it was impossible to make out their features, but O'Toole was downwind, and the breezes carried their voices easily.

They were speaking in a foreign language—several. One was completely unfamiliar to him, but he recognized the whispery guttural tones of German, the mellifluousness of French and an Oriental tongue that might have been Japanese. O'Toole understood none of it, save for two words that were uttered repeatedly with heavy accents: "Daytona" and "Orlando."

Several of the men began tampering with the locked doors at the rear of the truck. Suddenly they ran back. There was a blinding flash of blue and a hissing pop of plastic explosives. The men returned to the truck and the rear doors swung open.

Powerful flashlights were beamed inside and a hushed ceremony of congratulation took place with much back slapping. The pitch of their voices rose momentarily with their excitement. Again O'Toole heard the words repeated. Daytona. Orlando.

Bastards, O'Toole cursed silently. He raised his MAC-10 and sighted along the barrel at two of the terrorists, who stood back and watched the others unload crates of arms. How he would have loved to pull the trigger. He lowered the submachine gun. Not now. Not yet. His hungry impatience was tempered only by the certainty that the time to kill would come.

The dark, shadowy figures moved quickly, prying open a crate and examining the contents. Quickly it was moved to the trunk of the Toyota. A second crate was unpacked, and metal cases of ammunition were loaded into the Toyota's rear seat. The same procedure was followed to load the red Trans Am. One man stood back, examining a weapon that had been part of the shipment. O'Toole recognized the dark profile of an M-60 machine gun. Two other men appeared to be searching the undercarriage of the truck. He watched them, puzzled by their activity. With two cars, they could only hope to take a small fraction of the explosives and armaments from the secret shipment.

A light went on behind the windows of a Winnebago in the trailer park down the road, and an aluminum door slammed. The man with the M-60 quietly issued an order. The terrorists jumped for the cars. The headlights went on, and the drivers quickly backed out of the picnic area. The Trans Am braked abruptly before reaching the road. A man jumped from the cab of the truck and got in the Trans Am's passenger door.

Surprised by the suddenness of their departure, O'Toole backed into the swamp, feeling the cold dank water penetrate his boots. He had to get back to the car and Hayes fast. Instinctively he looked back. He saw the red taillights of the terrorists' cars turning onto the interstate ramp and the dark bulk of the abandoned diesel rig slowly moving forward, gaining speed as it headed straight for the Sleep-A-Wee Trailer Park.

Instantly the pieces of the puzzle came together in the mind of the Irish demolition expert. The men searching underneath the truck with its load of munitions had been planting explosives. The rig was a giant bomb, hurtling toward hundreds of innocent tourists sound asleep in their beds.

Liam O'Toole charged from the swamp, crashing through the underbrush onto the gravel parking lot, his legs kicking up dirt as he ran for the hell-bound rig. The distance closed as the Irishman ran faster on solid ground. The gears of the truck screamed with an ear-piercing shrillness as the tampered throttle pumped gas into the diesel engine. The truck pulled away, quickly gaining speed. Lights began to come on in windows of mobile homes in the trailer park. Doors slammed, and someone shouted. There was a scream and a curse.

"Oh my God, no!" O'Toole shouted, his ragged breath clawing at his lungs as he forced himself after the rapidly moving truck in a last all-out effort to overtake it.

The great metal beast bore down on the flimsy recreational vehicles like an anvil being lowered to crush pop cans.

"No!" Liam's cry was almost a sob. It was useless. It was more than useless. It was suicide.

The truck hit the first trailer, bashing it into the air and hurtling it against the next one, which in turn rolled against its neighbor.

O'Toole stopped, staring briefly, helplessly, as the trailers and campers fell like dominos in the truck's wake. There were shrieks of pain and surprise from people inside the doomed trailers. God help them, he thought, knowing what would happen next.

The diesel rig exploded in a flash of white light. Concussion waves slammed against him, hurtling him into the air and slapping him to the ground. He curled his body, pulling his arms around his head as a maelstrom of deadly debris blanketed him, ripping his clothing and tearing his skin. Suddenly the night was lit by a brilliant orange light from the fireball. Rapid pops of small explosions began as the flames detonated thousands of rounds of ammunition. O'Toole rolled over and over, the left side of his body, where he had hit the ground, in agony. His hands were sticky with blood from a head laceration he couldn't yet feel. He kept rolling farther and farther from the heat of the flames. The shrieks and screams of the dying and the panicked rent the air, punctuated by thunder bursts from exploding gas tanks. Fire spread like wind across water, flames falling onto the roofs of canvas tents, transforming them instantly into burning hell holes from which escape was impossible.

Liam O'Toole ignored his own pain and pulled himself to his feet. His head was swimming and blood flowed down his forehead into his eyes. He wiped it away. The quiet trailer park had been transformed into a hurricane of hell fire. It raged around the metal skeleton of the diesel rig. Bullets exploded by the caseload, firing indiscriminately in all directions. Some of them mercifully cut down the screaming human torches who were running among the flaming trailers and spreading the fire farther. For others, Sleep-A-Wee was sleep forever as they burned to death, trapped helplessly in their own beds.

He heard a car screeching down the ramp from the highway and turned to see the black Oldsmobile spinning across the picnic parking lot. Hayes braked inches from him and flung the passenger door open. O'Toole stumbled inside and fell against the seat. Hayes floored it and spun onto the road, heading back up the ramp, away from the terrible conflagration.

"Man, you look like hell," Hayes said grimly, his eyes on road as the speedometer climbed past a hundred and headed for one twenty.

O'Toole stopped to catch his breath. "What's happening in Daytona and Orlando, Claude?"

The black mercenary glanced curiously at O'Toole. "Funny you should say that. I relayed our position to Nate, and he told me those were the computer predictions. Orlando is a major tourist center. Wonderworld is there. The famous fairy-tale kingdom attracts tens of thousands a day, mostly families, lots of children. And Daytona is where the students go for their annual antics at spring break. Daytona Beach. The beer companies throw free rock concerts. Thousands of college kids are there this week.''

''That's where they're going. Daytona and Orlando.''

''Back there,'' Hayes said, his voice sharp with worry.''What . . . ?''

''What happened? That was just the preview, Claude. Just a preview of coming attractions.''

THE YACHT sheared the night in two, the side of the bow striking the cooler carrying the two men. Water poured in. The turbulence of the wake spun them around, and they pounded against the yacht's hull once more. Bishop grabbed Alex, wrapping an arm around his chest as the caved-in cooler floated bottom up in the Gulf of Mexico.

The waves closed over their heads, dragging Nanos away. Bishop reached under the water, grabbed Nanos's hair and held tight, pulling with his other hand to the surface. The high smooth hull of the yacht slashed the sea like a knife cutting jelly. It was virtually on top of him, battering his head. The wake washed against his face, covering his mouth and nose. His hand struck metal, jolting him with pain. With the final instincts of a drowning man, he grabbed for it.

It was the rung of a ladder.

The forward momentum of the yacht almost jerked his arm from its socket. He held on, pulled instantly to the surface, his other hand still clinging to Nanos's hair.

Using his legs as pinchers, Geoff Bishop gripped the Greek's torso and pulled him forward, securing a grip around his chest again. Alex was still breathing. The airman pushed the unconscious man in front of him and held on to the ladder with both hands. The ladder ran down the stern from the cockpit to below the waterline. The yacht was still gaining speed. The gathering velocity was pulling the slippery chrome bars from Bishop's fingers. There are times of crisis when human beings find themselves possessed of extraordinary reserves of strength and do extraordinary things. Mothers have single-handedly lifted cars off babies. Construction workers have lifted steel beams with their bare hands.

Somehow, exhausted as he was, with the wounded man in front of him and his arms reaching under Alex's armpits, Bishop climbed.

He climbed until they were almost halfway up the ladder, well out of the water. Then he reached around the steel struts and clasped Alex's wrists one at a time. He rested. He permitted himself to think about the bad dream that had suddenly descended on the two mercs. Pain racked his body. He promised himself that it would soon be over. Geoff Bishop thought about sleep. He thought about cool, white sheets, a soft bed and morning. He just had to take it step by step, and somewhere, somehow, an exit from the nightmare would appear, and he would take it. It would be over. Step by step.

The yacht was running blind in the night, skulking with its lights out, running from the explosion that had annihilated the Italian cruiser. The deck, two feet overhead, was barely visible in the darkness. Bishop looked up at it, knowing he had to climb to it and that what he found there might destroy him.

Alex Nanos's breathing was strong and regular. The Canadian merc contemplated taking his belt off and strapping the unconscious man to the ladder. Nanos stirred. His eyes were open. They met Bishop's, and the Canadian shook his head rapidly, warning the Greek not to speak. Nanos understood. Bishop moved his hands to the next rung and pulled. The Greek set his feet on the rung below them and pushed. Slowly, the two men climbed.

Just below the deck, Geoff Bishop gripped Alex's shoulder hard to stop him. He pulled himself past the Greek and carefully peered over the edge of the yacht.

The afterdeck was empty.

There was a very dim light glowing through the curtained window of a stateroom. Presumably there was someone on the bridge, driving.

Bishop retreated down the ladder to help Nanos. The man was half-conscious at best, his strength a fraction of what it should be. In the circumstances, every fraction helped.

Finally the two mercs sat on the deck of the yacht, their only cover the dark shroud of night. The Greek was on the verge of lapsing into unconsciousness again. His eyelids opened and closed, and his eyes rolled in his head.

Bishop put his arm under Nanos's shoulder and pulled him to his feet. Carefully, silently, the mercs moved forward, crossing the afterdeck to the starboard side of the superstructure where they were out of sight of the doors leading to the staterooms. Nanos sagged in Bishop's arms. Weakened critically by loss of blood, he was unable to maintain consciousness. With excruciating care to avoid the slightest noise, Geoff lowered Nanos to the deck below a stateroom window.

Again, for a few brief moments, the Canadian airman squatted on the deck to catch his breath, resting his head against the wall of the superstructure. His gut twisted into a knot of wires. At any moment, a gunman might turn a corner and spot them. His only weapon was his bare hands. Step by step, he reminded himself. Reconnaissance.

He could hear the thin vibration of muffled voices through the wall of the stateroom and raised his head to listen at the window. It was tightly curtained, but for a line of dim yellow light where two shutters came together.

The merc moved slowly, his bare feet silent on the yacht's midships deck. The sound of a man speaking grew louder as he came to an open window. The shutters had been partially closed, but there was a one-inch gap between them. Bishop pressed his eye to the opening and looked inside.

The stateroom was illuminated by a small night-light that was set in a wall sconce and partially obscured by a heavy shade. Two men sat on couches on either side of the salon. One, the man who had emerged from the speedboat with a message for the owner of the yacht, wore a windbreaker and loose-fitting pants. The other, a dark thickly bearded man in a business suit, sat with his shoulders hunched forward, straining to hear what the others said.

The man in the white suit who had appeared earlier on the bridge, stood at the bar, mixing drinks in a cocktail shaker. His movements were smooth and elegant, indicative of someone accustomed to wealth and power. The men's facial features were obscured by darkness, but Bishop had little doubt that he was witnessing the furtive face of a conspiracy—the leadership of the terrorist gangs set to ravage Florida.

The man in white handed a drink to the man on the couch and addressed him as Ron. They raised their glasses.

"To friends in high places—like the governor's office," Ron said, then sipped and set his glass down. He gestured toward the man with the thick beard. "Doesn't our buddy here drink?"

"Drink!" said the man in white. "He doesn't even speak English."

"No drringk," the bearded man said sharply. His English was thickly accented but he obviously understood. "Iss not my relisshun."

"Well, well. My mistake," the man in white said casually. "Drink up and toast farewell to this lovely old boat. Our rendezvous off Terra Ceia is in twenty minutes."

"Everything went quite smoothly until Washington sent this covert action team or whatever. Are they going to stop anything?"

"By ten o'clock this morning?" The man in white stood by the bar, tapping one of his fingers on the rim of his glass. "Uh-uh. No way. The Soldiers of Barrabas." He laughed in derision.

"The senator tells me this man Barrabas is someone to be reckoned with."

"I don't care what that lecherous cripple has to say. I tangled with Barrabas once before in these waters. But I was working with a bunch of amateurs, refugees from a 4-H rifles organization. The men I'm working with now are professionals. The most ruthless international terrorists in the world, motivated by a fanatical hatred toward America. They're highly trained, and they'll do anything. And the beauty of it is they can never be traced back to little old *moi.*"

Ron laughed. "A bit of an overstatement, isn't it? According to our friend, they've traced this yacht."

"And in a few short minutes, that will be taken care of."

"Still, you must admit it was a little foolish to be floating around the coast of Florida as the Liberian tanker deposited the submersibles."

The man in white shrugged. "I wanted to see."

"And after ten o'clock this morning? What then? You'll still have these mercenary soldiers to deal with."

"After ten o'clock this morning, they'll be completely discredited, my friend. The President will declare martial law and send in the military. Once the military has taken over as a domestic police force, certain friends of ours will ensure that they continue in that role for a long time to come. What will it take? Can you guess? A year? Six months? Three? Until we win the next presidential election? This country will see law and order as it has never seen law and order before. There will be demonstrations, riots, perhaps even insurrection—all deftly and ruthlessly quelled. And the unfortunate casualties of these terrible troubles will be the bleeding-heart liberals who weaken the will of America. Law and order. To preserve freedom, we must, for a time at least, deny it. An interesting irony."

"Well done."

"Yes, extremely well done. The operational principle is brilliantly simple. Use the existing framework. Harness the forces around you. And so, to organize a coup d'état in the United States, we utilize our enemies by unleashing them, provoking the nation to react. The reaction in turn unleashes tremendous public forces. We use those forces to take absolute control. The whole thing is done from within and so quietly that the great republic will never realize that democracy has been temporarily tampered with until, well . . . until it's been tampered."

"To the enemy within!" Ron raised his glass briefly and sipped again.

"An interesting turn of speech. But then to exist is to be someone's enemy, is it not? Like animals of the wild, we are carnivores, seeking smaller prey to devour, as we ourselves are sought by those who would devour us. Those who do not eat starve to death. Or are eaten." The man in white glanced sideways at his watch as he drained his glass.

"I would go on, but I'm tired, it's late, and we're running out of time," he said, reaching for a leather attaché case on a nearby table. He handed it to the man with the beard. "When we get to shore, one of my men will take you to the car. It's parked in a rest area near the entrance to the old Skyway Bridge. It's a big one, a silver Lincoln, and it's packed to the hilt with the most powerful explosives available. They require a large initial explosion to set them off. That's what the briefcase is for. You will be one of the first to drive your car to the top of the newly completed Sunshine Skyway. The opening ceremonies will have just finished, and the governor will have returned to the shore to watch the first cars complete the journey. You will take the briefcase, push on the clasps and put it in the back seat. The case will not open. It will blow up in one minute and detonate the explosives in the car. If you decide to run for it to save your own life, you will have one minute."

"Is not necessary," the bearded man hissed. "I die in holy war." He broke into a gleaming smile, and his eyes grew foggy in rapture. He pointed upward, nodding with assurance. "Paradise!"

"Well, it's up to you. I know what I would do." The man in white set his glass on the bar and turned to his friend. "The explosion will blow a hole in the Skyway, causing sufficient structural damage to collapse. The top section of the bridge will drop into the shark-filled water of Tampa Bay. All the cars driving over it will follow. *Voilà*. Catastrophe. Before the governor's own eyes. Think of how much Americans will want to see their governments show muscle to protect them from these terrible calamities. They will beg for martial law. And the governor, with his presidential ambitions and thankful for his own life, will be its midwife."

The man in white moved to an intercom near the bar and pressed a button.

"How are we doing up there?"

The grainy voice of the pilot emerged from the speaker.

"We have five minutes to rendezvous. The boat coming to meet us is visible now off the port side."

From his vantage point outside the stateroom, Geoff Bishop watched as the man in white spoke into the intercom again. A cold chill curled up his spine.

"Excellent." The yacht's owner turned to the other two men. "Well gentlemen, we must go. As captain of this yacht I hereby command, abandon ship!"

9

Even by dawn's early light, dark ladies of the night still wandered under the tinsel-town marquees of XXX-rated movie houses on Orange Blossom Trail. The sky was cloudless, promising its usual intensity of blue as the earth turned, revealing the sun like a neon orange on the eastern horizon.

Lee Hatton watched it rise from the cabin of the military helicopter flying over Orlando. She found herself wondering if somewhere a man who had been her lover also saw it. Or if Geoff Bishop was dead. Silently she cursed herself for her sentimentality, something she had always equated—unjustifiably—with feminine weakness. She tried to put him from her mind, but even as she made the effort, found herself hoping he was safe.

Billy Two placed his big callused hand on hers and squeezed. "He is somewhere. Do not be afraid," he said softly, his warm brown eyes sincere in his concern for her.

Lee forced herself to smile. She wasn't optimistic, but she had a gun, and she'd have her revenge. Maybe not directly from the guy responsible, but from one of his cohorts. She distracted herself by looking out the helicopter window.

Orlando, the fast-growing metropolis of central Florida, was visibly coming to life with the first glimmer of morning. Delta Force Major Landry Carter kept the chopper on a steady course, following Interstate 4 to Clear Lake, then detouring north to the East-West Expressway. Nate Beck continued to transmit from the command headquarters in Tampa.

"Red Dog calling Manatee. Over."

"Manatee reading. Over." Barrabas kept the mouthpiece near his lips as he watched the traffic begin to crowd the freeway a hundred feet below.

"Subjects westbound on East-West Expressway approaching eastern city limits. Speed constant at fifty-eight miles an hour. Over."

"Thank you, Red Dog. Manatee over and out." The colonel turned to Carter. "Let's follow the expressway east, and see if we can spot a green Toyota."

They had covered barely a mile when Nate came back on with an urgent transmission.

"Manatee, subjects have taken the exit at Highway 436, Semoran Boulevard, proceeding north into an area called Azalea Park. Over."

"Keep tracking, Red Dog. Manatee out. Major Carter, can this bird fly any faster?"

"Not unless she grows wings, Colonel."

"Colonel," Lee said, leaning forward from the rear cabin seat, "why don't we just use the chopper to stop them cold. If we come from the air, hit them straight from above, they won't know what's happening."

Barrabas shook his head. "We'd risk loosing a chance to find their headquarters here. There's probably a whole nest of them hiding out. No, we find the house and go in.''

"Just us?'' Billy Two asked. "Or with SWAT?''

"We get the first crack at them. We earned it. But Nate has instructions to inform Burton the moment we go in, and you can bet your ass he'll be there fast. Who knows, maybe we'll need the backup.''

"Not us,'' Billy Two said, folding his arms across his chest and glowering.

"I hope they're good shots and they pick their targets,'' said Lee, warily.

"Knowing Johnny Burton, the SWAT teams probably have instructions to pick us off first,'' Barrabas commented.

Billy Two shrugged, suddenly unconcerned. "No problem. The bigger the odds, the better we are.''

The others laughed, glad for the release of tension. In a sense it was true, too.

"Red Dog calling Manatee. Are you reading? Over.''

"Manatee reading, Red Dog. What's happening?''

"Get your map out. Subjects have turned east off Semoran Boulevard into Azalea Park, proceeding east on Hibiscus Avenue. It's a short street, Manatee, they may— Standby Manatee. Subjects appear to have stopped, and the satellite tracking signal is fading! They may be unloading the goods!''

"Thank you, Red Dog. Manatee out.'' Barrabas pulled the earphones from his head and lifted his MAC-10 into his lap. "End game!'' he shouted to the mercs. He checked the Sterling submachine gun's mag and quickly counted the spares in the pockets of his bulky windbreaker. As had the other mercs, Barrabas had donned a bullet-proof vest again, and his handgun was nestled in its holster under his left arm.

Soon the chopper passed the airport at Herndon Field, and closed in on the tree-lined streets of a quiet residential neighborhood.

The small frame bungalows had been built in the 1950s. Swimming pools shone like wide blue eyes from the midst of brightly colored shrubs in full flower. The mercs spotted the green Toyota in a driveway already crowded with parked cars. Men and women in drab green fatigues were unloading metal ammunition boxes and wooden crates containing arms.

"Manatee to Red Dog. Do you read me? Over."

"Red Dog reading, Manatee. Over."

"We're going in."

The words were barely out of his mouth when the wail of sirens rose in the distance. Barrabas craned to see past Landry Carter. A cavalcade of police vehicles, including SWAT vans, was raising dust down Semoran Boulevard.

"Damn!" Barrabas swore. "Damn, back out, Carter! That bastard Johnny Burton. He knows we're here! He's been monitoring our radio transmissions."

"I thought they were scrambled!" Landry Carter cried, angling the chopper away from the terrorist headquarters.

"So did I." Barrabas grabbed binoculars from the control panel and scanned the terrorists' lair. The sirens built to a screaming, anxious frenzy. The terrorists gathered beside the Toyota, looked in the direction of the noise. One of them pointed toward the helicopter.

"Let's go for it!" Barrabas screamed, throwing down the field glasses and reaching for his gun. Carter dropped the helicopter so fast that the mercs were lifted from their seats.

Like a bird of prey dropping from the sky, the chopper swooped over the house, its skids tearing shingles from the peak of the roof. The terrorists froze momentarily.

Doors on either side of the helicopter slid back, and the side of the bird bristled with the steel barrels of submachine guns. Fair warning. The killers scuttled in all directions like cockroaches caught in the sudden glare of a light bulb. Some fled across the lawn toward the cars. Others retreated into the house.

Windows shattered and gunfire erupted from the house as the helicopter hovered above the lawn in the front yard. The mercs returned fire as bullets spattered against the side of the chopper. Two of the terrorists danced in the frame of the living room picture window like puppets on a ten-foot television screen. The show was cancelled when they fell over the window sill into the garden and stopped moving. A white car ripped backward out the driveway just as the first of the police cars arrived on Hibiscus Street. The two vehicles collided like fists slamming into steel, turning vertically into the air and flipping. The white car was flattened. It rolled across the street and onto the lawn, landing upside down between the house and the helicopter. The mercs leaped out and ran toward the house, darting behind the cover of the demolished vehicle.

A SWAT van hit the overturned police car, and police on motorcycles swerved, their tires screeching as they barely avoided impact. Now the road was blocked. Two more of the terrorists' cars roared to life and veered into the street, racing past the smashed police vehicles.

SWAT shooters dropped to their knees, firing automatic rifles after the escaping terrorists. A withering fusillade of gunfire burst from the house again, dropping three police officers. Bullets chunked into the white car in front of the helicopter and whizzed past the mercs.

"Get back in!" Barrabas shouted, waving Hatton and Starfoot in a retreat across the lawn. "Carter, take us out of here and follow those cars!"

The chopper jerked upward as the mercs scrambled aboard, grabbing on to the seats for support. Below, the battle had settled into a stalemate between police hidden behind the wreckage of their cars and terrorists holed up in the house. A beautiful sunny day in the quiet neighborhood of Azalea Park had been riddled by a blizzard of bullets.

The escaping cars tore up the street in an easterly direction. The first, a pale blue Ford, turned right with breaking speed, and the second car, a new yellow Chrysler, followed. Their destination was obvious: the East-West Expressway, half a mile away. Once they were there, they could easily lose themselves in the rush-hour congestion. Even a helicopter assault would be dangerous, risking the lives of countless innocent people in the freeway traffic.

"Go for the blue car in front," Barrabas calmly instructed the Delta Force major at the controls. "That should slow the Chrysler down."

The cars carrying the terrorists in their flight swerved back and forth on Semoran Boulevard, pulling into the oncoming traffic to pass. The ear-splitting screams of rubber tires ripped across asphalt as cars veered quickly from the path of the terrorists.

Carter increased velocity, flying the chopper a tenth of a mile ahead of the blue car. He banked quickly into a one-hundred-and-eighty-degree turn.

"Wait for that clearing in the traffic," Barrabas told him, seeing that terrorists were headed for a quarter-mile stretch free of cars. The blue Ford hit the open stretch.

"Now!"

The Delta major took the helicopter down on a collision course with the Ford's windshield. At the final fraction of a second, he pulled back on the cyclic control, reversing the chopper's direction and narrowly averting a collision. The driver of the blue Ford panicked and hit the brakes. His tires smoked on the pavement, and the car's rear end fishtailed, pulling the car counterclockwise in a full circle and directly into the path of the yellow Chrysler.

The second car veered right, clipping the Ford behind its front fender. Lee Hatton leaned from the door of the chopper with her MAC-10 and let it rip. Bullets pounded through the Ford's hood, and its radiator blew geysers of steam. The barrel of an automatic rifle appeared from the passenger window. Carter angled the chopper into battle position, protecting its underside, where delicate lines carried hydraulic fluid and fuel to vital mechanisms.

The Ford ground to a halt, its tires flattened and clouds of steam hissing from the front grill. A pool of leaking gasoline and oil oozed quickly from underneath the car. The front doors swung open as the terrorists attempted to escape the crippled vehicle.

"Control fire!" Barrabas shouted, as the two men hit the road. He spun a three-round burst into the asphalt inches from the driver's feet, driving him back toward the car. Billy Two opened up on the second man from the other side.

Civilian traffic proceeding toward the battle scene slowed with initial curiosity. Several cars braked and pulled to the side of the road. Drivers began to panic, trying to turn their cars to flee in the opposite direction. Within seconds, cars were locked tight in a knot that blocked the road. The impatient driver of a black Dart geared up, speeding along the soft shoulder in a trail of dust.

The terrorists retreated toward their car as the helicopter circled slowly, hovering with the tail boom and the antitorque rotor pointed away from the gunfire, and the bullet-proof cockpit facing the conflict. The mercs continued to pound three-round bursts into the ground, corralling the escaping men against the Ford.

Suddenly one of them turned, loosing a stream of autofire at the black Dart as it roared past. The driver lost control. The car swerved and tipped onto the road, scraping up the highway on its side, its roof smashing into oncoming traffic. Cars spilled sideways off the road.

The other terrorist emerged from the Ford, aiming his automatic rifle in the direction of the stalled traffic. The butchers opened up on the innocent people trapped in the cars around them. Lead splattered into windshields, killing the occupants of the front seats immediately. People rushed hysterically from their cars in a last-ditch effort to flee. Ruthlessly the terrorists turned their guns and mowed them down.

The mercs had no choice, faced with the cold-blooded slaughter below. Barrabas, Starfoot and Hatton aimed the barrels of their weapons and held the triggers. They cut down the terrorists, their bullets punching into the killers, hurling them away from the cars. The first one died immediately, his heart exploding through his chest in a shower of blood. The second faltered, fell to one knee, raised his gun and fired weakly at the chopper.

Barrabas aimed quickly, pulling the trigger once. The terrorist's head jerked, the side of his skull shattered. For a moment, he remained frozen in position. Then slowly he collapsed, blood spreading in a pool under his body.

A heavy silence floated over the carnage on the road, almost overwhelming the steady grind of the chopper's engines. Then it was joined by screams and hysterical weeping from the innocent whose only crime was to be driving in the wrong place at a very bad time. Once again, sirens sounded in the distance.

"The other car!" Barrabas said, twisting in his seat to survey the road.

Carter steadied the chopper, and moved it forward over the roadside killing ground.

In the bloody melee, the yellow Chrysler had successfully eluded them.

"ANOTHER STUDENT has plunged to his death after a drunken spree of balcony hopping in Daytona Beach.

Roderick Beschneidet, a University of Oklahoma sophomore, misjudged his distance or lost his balance while attempting to jump to the balcony adjacent to his room at the Playa Monda Hotel. He fell thirteen stories to the swimming pool deck, where…''

Claude Hayes switched off the car radio and turned to Liam O'Toole in the driver's seat. ''Man, what is going on here? I feel like we just landed on Bizarro World.''

''More like Planet of the Apes. America's youth is letting it all hang out,'' the Irish-born merc sighed, his eyes glued to the car with Illinois license plates ahead of him, where five buxom blondes wearing Party Naked T-shirts waved from the windows.

''Hey you!'' O'Toole stuck his head out the window and yelled. ''Get out of there!''

An overweight kid with a baseball cap on backward ran into the street sticking Life is a Beach bumper stickers on every car that went by. He stopped, poised to strike at the mercs' windshield.

''Go on! I said, get!''

One look at O'Toole's face was enough to dissuade him. He stuck out his tongue and scampered off in pursuit of more congenial targets.

The mercs had been caught in bumper-to-bumper traffic on the main highway leading from the Interstate into Daytona Beach. The morning sun had risen on thousands of college kids arriving from the north to join tens of thousands of others on their winter break. It was a little after 9:00 a.m., and already they were turning the town upside down. The digital readout on the dashboard produced a steady stream of updates on the location of the Trans Am. At the moment it was not far ahead of them, stuck in the same immense traffic jam.

"Yeah, but jumping off balconies!" The insanity of it was beyond Claude Hayes's comprehension.

"Well, they don't jump off, Claude. They fall. You know—they get a little tanked up and decide to play follow the leader. Every year down here a half dozen of so don't make it. They go bye-bye and splat. Look at it this way, it's survival of the fittest. I mean, if they're that stupid in the first place, it gets them out of the way before they're a danger to the rest of us."

"Brother, I hear you."

O'Toole struggled with the heavy traffic for another forty minutes until they had crossed the causeway over the Halifax River. Daytona Beach was little more than a giant honky-tonk covering a long sandspit. The boardwalk was a strip of pavement leading past pinball arcades and miniature-golf courses with plastic dinosaurs and pink elephants. Half a dozen high-rise hotels dotted the seashore, with a surplus of low-rise motels and bars in between.

When they got close to the seashore, their progress was slow enough for Claude Hayes to leave the car and trail the Trans Am on foot. He moved ahead, looking for the red car. Finally he saw it locked in traffic less than a quarter mile ahead of them. The black man moved into position halfway between it and the Oldsmobile.

O'Toole stayed in the traffic, which streamed steadily down a hill and under a stone gate. To his astonishment, directly in front of him, the wild Atlantic surf foamed onto the strand. He had driven onto one of the wide sandy beaches that ran for miles along

Florida's east coast. On his right, a pier with a restaurant and observation tower jutted into the water. The traffic led to the left.

Two rows of parked cars stretched along the tawny sand as far as the eye could see, and a slow-moving avenue had formed between them. The spectacle going on around him was half carnival and half freak show.

Oiled, nearly naked bodies sprawled across the hoods of cars and lounged in the open side doors of custom vans. The boys and girls of American academe wandered among the vehicles, strutting their stuff as if it was merchandise in a Damascus flea market. It was cruise city, and O'Toole wasn't referring to the traffic.

One enterprising young man with a Polaroid camera had a hand-lettered sign on top of his van that read, Buns Gallery, and on the side of the van, there were dozens of photos of female derrieres. Young ladies were lining up for the honor of adding theirs to his collection. A bearded man wearing multiple layers of heavy clothing paraded with a sign that read, Repent in the Raw—Nudist Christian Church.

A little farther on, a blond sophomore in mirrored aviator glasses held a sheet of cardboard announcing Free Advice.

"Come over here, little lady, tell me your problems," he barked. "Now what I suggest, and I guarantee this will solve your problems, is that you spend a few minutes with me at the motel and . . ."

"Jeez," O'Toole muttered. "Alex Nanos would go wild at this party." Suddenly a long slender arm reached in the window and fingers ran through his hair. His eyes were confronted by the sight of perfectly formed breasts barely held back by a spandex bikini.

"Hey redhead, is your hair that color all over?" She had long black hair and saucy eyes. In her free hand she clutched a can of beer in a Styrofoam insulation cup. "Prove it!"

"Love to baby, but maybe later. . . ."

"Got someone else?" she said petulantly. "I don't see them."

"No. No, honest . . ."

But already the babe had lost interest. She leaped away, shrieking, "Party naked! Eeeeeee!" and ripped the skimpy bikini from her breasts. A great chorus of shrieks, cheers, applause and animalistic mating noises ensued as she danced down the line of cars, swinging her bra and spraying her fans with beer.

"Whew!" The merc exclaimed, suddenly sweating under his jacket. Hayes ran to the window.

"Hey man, the dude found a parking space and he's leaving the Trans Am on the beach."

"What's he doing? That car is loaded with explosives."

"I dunno, man. He hasn't had time to wire it yet. But we better keep our eye on him. Can you park this thing?"

"Where?"

The two men looked quickly up and down the beach. The Oldsmobile was locked between two solid rows of parked cars, and the line of traffic ran at least three miles before there was a way out.

"Here." O'Toole grabbed a wallet from inside his windbreaker and flipped a wad of hundred dollar bills to Hayes. "Buy a parking space."

Hayes walked over to three young men coating themselves with grease on the hood of a Pacer. He offered them a hundred. They hesitated. He upped it to two. After a brief conference, they accepted. The merc shoved the rest of the wad back at O'Toole. The Pacer pulled out and the Irishman drove in.

"Come on, he's heading off the beach," Hayes said, craning his neck to keep the man in view. The terrorist was a thin man of medium height, with short wiry hair and a long handlebar moustache. His skin was dark, possibly Mediterranean. He walked quickly across the sand, a dour, unsmiling expression on his face. He looked constantly left and right, turning his head back over his shoulder and squinting to see ahead of him. Like the two mercs, he wore a bulky windbreaker. Neither Claude Hayes nor Liam O'Toole had any illusions about what was underneath it.

"Come on, this way," Hayes grabbed O'Toole's arm, steering him toward the boardwalk on a path across the beach that paralleled the terrorist's. "We gotta keep our distance, cause this dude is real paranoid."

"It's what he's got to be paranoid about that worries me."

"We'll find out, Liam. Real soon."

The whirrs and ringing bells of the pinball arcades flooded through open glass doors onto the crowded boardwalk. Thousands had begun to gather at the site of an open-air rock concert sponsored by one of the big breweries. Technicians used a small crane to lower giant speakers and adjusted audio on the huge outdoor stage. In another hour, some forty thousand people would be concentrated on the strip.

The terrorist pushed through the throngs of festive young people, hastily making his way toward the far end of the asphalt strip. The mob thinned past the concert area, where a modern fifteen-story hotel jutted onto the beach. The man quickened his pace in that direction.

Confronted by the oncoming multitudes pouring onto the beach to hear the concert, Hayes and O'Toole lost sight of their quarry. They broke into a run, slamming into people and twisting sideways to slip through the crowds. Shouts and rude epithets followed them as they made their way to the edge of the crowd. The terrorist dashed inside the front door of the hotel.

Hayes and O'Toole quickly darted in and out of the pedestrian traffic. Some students had hung a bed sheet with the words Free Jumping Lessons on it from a third-floor balcony. A couple of fast-talking New York photographers, armed with hundreds of pounds of lenses, Hasselblads and tripods, milled about below. They shouted encouragement to the students on the balcony while security guards ordered the students to take down the sign.

"Come on, go higher and start jumping," a photographer shouted.

"Give us a show, man."

"Let's see someone fall!"

A short wiry man with a beard stumbled in front of the two mercs, a camera larger than his head pressed to his eye.

"Sorry, pal," he said, smiling apologetically, rushing his words in blind excitement. "Oh man, all I need is a pic of one falling student to make my career. I can sell it for at least a hundred grand in exclusive international rights." He ran under the balcony, shouting, "Jump! Jump! What, are you scared or something? Come on, give me a fatal plunge!"

By the time the mercs reached the lobby, the terrorist had disappeared. O'Toole went to the desk and beckoned to the clerk. His heart pounded.

"My friend just came in. I got hung up in the crowd outside. He got ahead of me, and I forget the room number. You know the guy. He just came by here— short, about your height, dark hair, moustache. Foreigner. Drives a red Trans Am."

"Ah, Mr. Ricotti. He's about the only normal guest we have left since the students took over."

"Yeah, Rabid Ricotti. That's what we call him. A nickname, huh. What's the room number again?"

"Nine thirty-eight."

"Thanks buddy. You made my day."

The mercs rushed to the bank of elevators. The doors opened, and a wave of whooping, hollering students in beach gear pushed forth, surged around them and flowed into the lobby. Hayes and O'Toole jostled through the other people waiting to go up.

Hayes pressed nine.

O'Toole planted himself in the door and put out his arms to push back the people trying to crowd on.

"Sorry, this car's taken."

"Hey!" someone in the crowd shouted amid a chorus of objections. "You can't—"

"Oh yes, I—" the doors slid shut "—can." The Irishman reached inside his windbreaker and pulled out his handgun.

"Remember, we're supposed to take prisoners." Hayes took a similar gun from his concealed shoulder holster.

"Oh, you know me, Claude," Liam mused, releasing the safety catch at the rear of the grip. "I'm always ready to take prisoners. But after all, it's up to the other guy, too."

The elevator stopped. Cautiously Hayes peered outside the doors. The corridor was empty.

The two men slipped down the hall. Room nine thirty-eight was a corner room facing the ocean beaches and the boardwalk. For a moment, they stood outside the door, listening. They heard metal clunking against metal. The mercs looked at each other. O'Toole carefully tried the handle. It was bolted. He aimed his gun at the lock and nodded to Hayes.

The big black man backed up and raised his foot. The flimsy hotel lock shattered with the impact of the steel-toed boot. The door bounced open half a foot, arrested by a night bolt.

O'Toole fired, blowing the chain to bits.

"Freeze! Don't move or I'll blow your head off!" the mercs shouted as they burst inside.

The interior of the hotel room looked like a bunker. A double line of mortars, linked in a series by heavy cables, was aimed out the open windows in a direct line to the throngs gathering for the rock concert. The terrorist from the Trans Am stood inside the balcony door, aiming a portable launcher at the beach. A second one had been fiddling with some wires leading from bundles of plastic explosives. He held an electric detonator in one hand. Incendiary rockets lay in open boxes stacked up the walls.

For a split second the terrorists froze. The man on the balcony looked at the mercs, then turned to aim his launcher. The other one raised the detonator.

"Drop it!" Hayes shouted, swinging his gun arm into line with the man with the plastics. The terrorist obliged. His eyes bulged wide and white with messianic fanaticism. Screaming like a banshee, he threw himself bodily at the black merc, grabbing Hayes's gun by the barrel. O'Toole aimed at the man on the balcony and fired. The bullet caught the side of the launcher. It flew from the assassin's hand and landed on the balcony.

"You move, you die!" the Irishman shouted, racing across the room.

The terrorist looked at the red-haired fury rushing him. He turned and without a backward glance, leaped over the edge of the balcony into thin air.

10

Crouched under the stateroom window, Geoff Bishop noticed the early glimmer of light on the eastern horizon that heralded the approach of day. The distant whine of an outboard engine grew louder. St. Petersburg glowed among the keys to the north. Night had faded only slightly, but a dark coastline was visible less than half a mile to the south. The grand arch of the new Sunshine Skyway soared across the water beside the rusting iron girders of the old one barely a few hundred yards off the side of the yacht.

They had not moved very far from their earlier position off Egmont Key—perhaps five miles. The motorboat was approaching from the bay to the south, Terra Ceia. Closer, the causeway approach to the Skyway snaked over the land and across the shallow entrance of Tampa Bay.

Alex Nanos moaned, sending a chill of fear through Bishop. The three men in the stateroom had stood and were at the door leading to the aft deck. The footsteps of the pilot clattered on the ladder from the bridge.

The mercs had no cover, no protection except the shade of night, and that was rapidly disappearing.

Bishop squatted beside Nanos. He stared at Bishop, his dark eyes riveted on the airman's face.

Geoff placed a finger lightly to his lips. He met the Greek's eyes. Nanos didn't move, but he understood. Bishop cupped his arms under Nanos's knees and shoulders and lifted him. Stepping as quickly as he dared, he carried the man toward the bow.

The men aboard the yacht had congregated on the deck outside the stateroom. The high-speed launch was twenty yards off the side of the boat. The bridge, with its high glass windows, loomed above Bishop. The roof of a cabin, meeting the bridge, rose shoulder-high. He set Nanos down and crouched beside him. Activity aboard the yacht would be concentrated in the stern. The only advantage they had, other than the thinning darkness of night, was that they were presumed dead. There was no reason for anyone to walk to the bow of the yacht. If they did... Bishop looked at his bare hands.

The conversation among the sinister men was boisterous. There were loud guffaws and laughter. Silence. The murmur of words and more laughter, less interested. They were waiting for something.

A retching vibration shuddered through the hull of the yacht and disappeared. Voices rose on the stern. They were stepping off one by one.

Bishop waited, hardly breathing, listening for the sounds that would somehow dictate his next course of action. Step by step. One at a time. If only the pilot was left aboard, it would be simple, he thought. Even two would be easy to kill.

The launch pushed away and sped across the water, the engine drone winding away in the wind. Bishop listened for the sound of footsteps.

Silence.

He waited, fighting the illusion of time passing by counting, adding the seconds into minutes and waiting for five of them. He had gone past his threshold of fatigue into the adrenaline zone of inexhaustible energy. But he also knew that if he stopped—even just to think—he'd crash. He'd collapse.

Alex Nanos continued to stare at him intently, without uttering a word or even moving.

"Wait here, old buddy," Bishop whispered.

He stood. The eastern sky was tinged with orange just at the horizon. The sleek expensive lines of the boat were abandoned.

Bishop moved slowly along the side to the stern. The cabin door swung open, and the stateroom was dark and empty. Stepping softly, he ascended the steps to the bridge, slipping along the upper deck until he could look sideways through the windows. The bridge was deserted.

It was not the realization that they had abandoned ship that made Bishop's gut twist. It was the unknown reason.

He took an ax from a case marked Fire. There would be time to search for a firearm later. He descended to the stateroom and turned on a lamp. The dark wood-paneled room with its brass fittings and leather upholstery was expensive, elegant and empty save for three cocktail glasses and a few butts in an ashtray.

From deep within the ship came a strange gurgling whisper. Several steps led down to a corridor. Rushing, foaming water poured from the head, surging over the carpet and lapping at the steps.

The yacht had been scuttled. The through-hull fittings were smashed beyond repair, and the ocean poured through the rupture. The ship lurched suddenly in the water, tilting slightly to one side, and the lights flickered. Once the engine compartments were flooded, the current would die. The yacht would sink fast, and it would suck him and Nanos to the bottom with it.

Geoff Bishop raced onto the deck and climbed to the bridge again. He tore open the cupboards under the control panel, finding rolls of nautical charts and a windbreaker. He put the jacket on over his bare chest, remembering compartments built into the superstructure at deck level.

He found them locked, raised the ax and smashed the fiberglass doors to pieces. In a compartment at the stern, he found what he was looking for. An emergency inflatable dinghy. Even as the sky turned royal blue, fluted at the eastern edge with flamingo pink, the rolling waters heaved metallic gray and the yacht lurched again, sinking deeper and listing to port. Working feverishly, Bishop spread the deflated rubber and broke the seal on the pressurized gas. Instantly the dinghy began to inflate. They had to be at least fifty feet from the yacht when it went under to avoid the whirlpool of suction.

He ran to the bow, where Nanos waited, still conscious. "Boat's sinking. We gotta go." The Canadian airman knelt to lift Nanos, but the Greek pushed him away, trying to stand. Weakened by the loss of blood, he lurched and fell against his rescuer.

"It's okay, Alex. Lean on me," Bishop said, throwing Alex's arm over his shoulder and standing. They made their way to the aft deck, Nanos half walking and half dragged. Water had risen over the stateroom floor and flowed onto the deck. Every minute the list worsened, making movement more difficult. Even the modest exertion drained Nanos. By the time they reached the stern, he had lapsed into unconsciousness again, his weight slumping heavily against Bishop.

Wordlessly the airman put the dinghy in the water. He found some blankets sealed in plastic in the deck compartment and threw them down. Putting his shoulder into Nanos's midriff, he took the Greek in an over-the-shoulder carry and backed carefully down the ladder.

He laid Nanos carefully on the floor of the small inflated boat and threw a blanket over him before using the aluminum paddle to push away from the yacht. The water along the hull bubbled as the stern fell lower, and water poured over one corner onto the aft deck. The more it sank, the faster it went. Bishop paddled, the strong and steady movements second nature to him, a skill honed on the white-water rivers of northern forests. The wind had risen, blowing against him off the land. The waves were higher. He sweated, paddling until his arms ached and blisters began to burn his bare wet hands.

For a long time, he didn't look back. The sea behind him gurgled so sharply that it might have snapped open. Then the water fizzed and bubbled as it closed together, swallowing the luxury yacht in a single gulp.

When Bishop finally turned, there was no trace of the yacht, the surrounding waves not even scarred from the disturbance.

The morning sun rose majestically over Tampa Bay, an orb of scalding gold, burnishing with liquid pink the steel webbing of the new Skyway Bridge. The sea was baby blue, heaving like a silk banner ruffled in a breeze. He was a mile offshore, paddling against the wind, and the current promised to sweep him under the bridge. He kept paddling, oblivious to the pain mounting in his arms and back and to the sweat that soaked his skin and ran into his eyes.

The torturous journey would be over only if he took it step by step. He had to stop an assassin about to slaughter hundreds of innocent people. Nanos needed medical attention. Only Bishop knew of the secret conspiracy, of the sharp-toothed jackals who would turn the country into a corpse and gnaw at its bones. Geoff Bishop had seen the enemy within. He had to live—to tell.

BARRABAS GRABBED THE RADIO and spoke rapidly, "Manatee calling Red Dog. Do you read? Over."

"Red Dog reading. Over."

"Get me clearance on the police channels, Red Dog. I want to talk to Burton. Over."

The words were barely out of his mouth when an immense explosion reverberated over the roofs of the quiet suburban neighborhood. Shock waves pummeled the helicopter, and a perfect fireball roared up from the terrorists' hideout.

Sirens shrieked from every direction as police cars, ambulances and fire trucks poured into the area.

"I hope Johnny Burton checked for booby traps before he tried going in," Barrabas cracked cynically. The fashion-conscious detective was responsible for the getaway of the Chrysler and the slaughter on the road below. But Barrabas knew that when the fingers started pointing, they'd be pointed at him. And the SOBs didn't even have the legitimacy to clear themselves. "Take us over the expressway," Barrabas instructed the Delta Force pilot. "Let's see if we can spot the Chrysler."

A moment later, Johnny Burton's voice crackled over the police band. The agent from the state attorney general's office sounded whiny. Thick plumes of dark smoke rose from the direction of Azalea Park.

"Was the big boom a surprise, Burton?" Barrabas asked.

"It's no joke. I've got eight missing men, four dead and no one knows what's happening to the occupants of the adjacent houses that caught fire."

"Does that mean you didn't take prisoners?"

The radio was silent. Finally Burton spoke again.

"Cut the crap, Barrabas. We got a problem."

"My major problem is you, Burton. If you hadn't moved in like Patton's army, I wouldn't be worrying about the ones that got away."

"What do you want me to do?"

"Put out an APB on a light yellow recent-make Chrysler sedan. Four door. Probably on the East-West Expressway. I want every cop in Orlando looking, I want to know the reported locations of every one of them, and I want them all stopped."

"You got it Barrabas. Have fun."

"Oh, I'll have fun, Johnny. You're the one who has to clean up the mess. Over and out."

WALKER JESSUP WATCHED as the thin, bug-eyed man with spidery fingers used tweezers to hold the small slip of yellow paper to a light board. He wore optical enhancers with rows of sliding lenses over the bridge of his nose like a pair of glasses, lending an extraterrestrial appearance to his round face.

Albert Randome was an expert with the criminal investigation bureau of the Florida State Police in St. Petersburg, specializing in forgery and counterfeiting. If a crime involved ink, paper or a combination thereof, the evidence was brought to him.

"There are watermarks," the scientist said. "Very faint but unmistakable." He set the numbered stub down and took the glasses off. His eyes bulged from their sockets, extruding almost as far as his short pointed nose. He looked like an extremely intelligent insect.

"Theater ticket?" Jessup suggested.

Randome shook his head. "Better quality paper than your average ticket stub. It was printed by ACME Kwick Print, a Miami outfit. Unmistakable. Watermarks can seldom be confused."

"Call them," Jessup said excitedly, pointing to the telephone.

Albert Randome checked a card file and pushed the number. A few moments later he was talking to his contact in the Miami office of the printing company.

"It's printed on buff number four stock. Red lettering, two inches long and an inch wide. Number

H44438 in red ink, with a perforation on the right side only. Yes, right away. Very important. Yes, life and death. No, I'll hold.''

He looked up from the phone and nodded at Jessup with a satisfied smile. The Texan paced nervously, casting anxious looks periodically at Randome as they waited. The scientist's face suddenly beamed with happiness.

"Great!" he said into the phone. "Wonderful! Excellent! Let me write it down." He scribbled on a nearby notepad, hung up the phone and handed the slip of paper to Walker Jessup.

"Central Florida Costume Rentals in Orlando."

Jessup looked at him, then at the yellow stub. "From a costume rental?"

"Phone them," Albert Randome suggested, turning the telephone around to face Jessup.

The Texan dialed the number. A woman answered.

"Central Florida Costume Rentals, official suppliers of costumes and make up to Wonderworld. Can I help you?"

"I rented some costumes recently, and one of them is due back, but I can't remember which of them it is."

"Do you have a number?"

"Uh, sure. H triple four thirty-eight."

The woman left the phone, returning in less than a minute.

"That was one of our extended rentals, since you're an employee at Wonderworld. It's not due back until you terminate your employment. Have you stopped working?"

"Oh," Jessup said, momentarily disconcerted. "Uh, that was, uh, what costume was it? I rented several and I'm sure one of them is due back "

"That was the bear costume."

"The bear costume."

"Yes. For Goldilocks and the Three Bears, I believe. For Dream Land. At Wonderworld."

"That's right. Now I remember. Thanks very much for all your help." Jessup put down the telephone. He looked at the bug-eyed little man, his face aghast.

"Trouble?" Randome asked.

"Big."

The Texan ran from the laboratory before the scientist could open his mouth to question him further.

"RAH RAH RAH! Sis boom bah! Wonderworld Wonderworld hoooo-rah!"

The all-American type in a football sweater led the cheer while four identical blondes with batons and short skirts went through the motions.

"Golly, that was great girls. Let's run through it one more time with all the animals. Then we'll go out and hit them." The young man jabbed his fist into the air to punctuate his enthusiasm.

"Ah, Jason," one of the blondes whined, "lighten up, will ya! We have to go through this ridiculous cheer forty-eight times today, every fifteen minutes, out there at the main gates to Wonderworld. Enough is enough. Forget it girls. Let's go." She waved to the others and they jumped, eager to exit the dressing room.

"Do it with the animals," one of them teased as they left in a cloud of laughter. Jason really hated it when people didn't take their work seriously. Especially when they were lucky enough to have a wonderful job at Wonderworld, America's fantasy playground for the whole family.

Around him, actors and actresses slipped into change rooms or sat before mirrors to transform themselves into one of the many creatures of legend and lore that inhabited the Enchanted Kingdom and one of its four realms: Action Land, Pioneer Land, Dream Land and Future Land.

They emerged as cowboys and Indians, pirates and adventurers, South Seas natives, androids and robots and loveable, cuddly animals right out of Mother Goose and all the fairy tales. Hansel and Gretel painted freckles on their cheeks. Little Bo Peep carefully arranged her pony tails.

A white collar man wearing a dark tie appeared at the door. "Let's gooo! Five minutes until opening," he shouted, with managerial authority. "Hey, where are the Ugly Duckling and the five swans? They not here yet?"

A mild murmur of disinterest moved among the busy actors. No one spoke up.

"Hey, you over there," the manager yelled at a dark-haired man taking his costume from a locker. "Yeah, you, I forget your name. You're a friend of that guy aren't you. You know, the Ugly Duckling. Where's your buddy?"

The man at the locker shrugged. "Beats me. Hey, I hardly know the guy. I just talk to him, that's all."

The manager, skilled at distrusting employees, made a mental note of the actor's answer. "Well, you see him, you tell him to beat his hind end to my office, at the service entrance of Dracula's castle. He and the swans are in big trouble.'' He shook his clipboard to emphasize his seriousness. "We can't have this at Wonderworld. Now hurry up in here!''

The manager left amid a disinterested murmur of assent.

Hiding behind the door of his locker, Michael "Moonlight" Megarry snorted a bit of the white powder that helped him get through the day, every day, as Walter the Giant Penguin. In real life, he was a video performance artist from Toronto, forced to take work to support himself. He hated people who took their jobs seriously. Dick Dash, the manager, for instance, and Jason the Jock, all-American bore, who was striding in his direction. Elran, the dark-haired man who knew the Ugly Duckling, had the locker beside him.

"Take it easy, Elran," Megarry said, dropping the giant beak over his face. "To the front!" He pointed a wing and walked.

"Yah, take it easy. You too, yah," the man shouted after him, his voice dropping cynically as the giant penguin waddled out of hearing.

He was young, clean shaven and dark, his short hair black and tightly curled, but his eyes blue. The video artist from Toronto knew him as Elran, though that was not his real name. Elran threw his jacket into the locker and bent to take off his shoes. A giant bear costume lay on the bench behind him.

"Hey guys!" Jason appeared at his elbow. "All the animals have to know the Wonderworld 'Royal Razz' and be prepared to lead it or join in at any time. Let's just run through . . ."

Elran looked carefully to his right, his eyes cautioning the actors at the lockers nearby.

"We know it already," he said to Jason in a clearly hostile tone of voice.

"Aw, c'mon now. And you guys, too." Jason waved his hand at the others. They ignored him, taking off their shoes and pulling on bear boots in studied silence.

"None of you ever join in. You know, I'm going to report y'all to Mr. Dash. You're still on your three-month probation period, and you don't take your work very seriously."

Elran slammed the door of his locker shut and turned, his nose an inch from Jason's surprised face.

"Seriously? We take our work very seriously. Very, very seriously."

Jason drew back. "You do?"

"Yes." The man leaned into the American, jabbing a finger into his chest. "And I tell you what. We will lead all the Wonderworld animals in the 'Royal Razz' in Dream Land."

"You will?"

"Yes." Elran nodded generously, laughing. "And they will help." He pointed to his friends, a woman and a man, who zipped up their bear suits. One was a mommy bear, the other, a daddy bear. Another woman arranged the voluminous folds of her old-fashioned dress over wire hoops and carefully lifted a wig of long golden hair.

"At ten o'clock," Elran continued, "I will put you in charge of telling all the others, so we can meet there and do it together."

"Gee! What a great idea!" Jason began, backing away, clearly enthusiastic. "I'll spread the word, Elran. You can count on me." He waved and headed off.

The number of actors in the dressing rooms diminished substantially as the hands of the clock neared 9:30 a.m.—opening time. Sinbad and a number of scantily clad genies were near the door, laughing over a joke. A tall carrot with two legs helped an apple adjust its stem in front of the mirrors.

The woman dressed as Goldilocks sauntered toward Elran as he checked out the special straps he had sewn inside the bear suit. Her hair was so blond that it was almost white. Her skin was pale, drawn tightly across her cheek bones, assisted once, in the past, by a plastic surgeon's scalpel.

"I can count on him." Elran, gestured with his head at Jason as he disappeared. He smiled knowingly at the woman, whose name was Ingrid.

"But can we count on Hammer and the others? That cell—none of them has arrived!"

"Shh!" The dark-haired man cautioned her as Momma and Poppa Bear joined the conversation. He spoke rapidly to all of them in a low voice. "There is nothing we can do except to continue as planned."

"They've been stopped!" said the other man, a big Briton named Rayo.

"Probably," Elran answered. "They're hunting us down, and perhaps they are succeeding here and there. We knew that not all of us would reach our goals. But we also knew there were enough of us for some to survive. Let them throw all their might and all their fury against us. But they cannot stop us, for we shall come upon them as a swarm of flies upon a corpse, and we shall feed and multiply. And they shall know a terror that they have imagined only in their wildest dreams or darkest fantasies. My brother and sisters, only we are left. So we must do it alone. Are you ready?''

They nodded. The two bears placed their heavy hollow bear heads on. Elran carefully lifted the nine-millimeter submachine gun from his locker and placed it in the Velcro loops in one side of his costume. He took a belt studded with spare magazines, and hid it in the other side.

Goldilocks clutched a wicker basket filled with flowers. ''Remember, my friends, I will be fleeing with the crowd from your bullets. Be sure not to hit me. Or else I will not be able to set off these explosives in the middle of the panicked mob.''

Elran tapped his fist against his bear head. It was lined with steel. He smiled at the reassuring feel of metal, and placed it over his head. A bullet-proof vest had been sewn inside his costume. He personally had made the alterations, unknown to his fellow terrorists. They understood it was a suicide mission. Elran had no intention of dying.

''How do I look?'' he asked, his voice muffled.

''Like my widdo widdo Baby Bear!'' Momma Bear answered in a sing-song voice, patting him on the head with her great furry paw.

''Come on, you guys, you're three minutes late!'' Dick Dash was at the door. ''Let's get out there. The happy world of Wonderworld awaits the wondering world of world-weary tourists. They need you! Let's give it to them!''

It was the moment Elran had waited for, the moment of the most brilliantly planned and the most exceptionally shocking act of terrorism ever to be perpetrated on United States soil—in the very center of its national playground, in Wonderworld, the heart of the American dream come true.

They came here to drug themselves on play and happiness, adults indulging in infantile joys. For camera-laden convoys of parents with children, it was a pilgrimage, an event of great significance to the life of the nuclear family. It symbolized the carefree rewards of fantasy, the fruit of dreams. It was the factory of the American imagination.

Goldilocks and the Three Bears skipped down the path that led into the Magic Forest, near the gates of the Enchanted Kingdom. Already, visitors flooded through the grounds rushing to chosen rides and pavilions, anxious to be first in the fast-growing line-ups. Hidden loudspeakers played merry polka music, and giant furry animals danced under the synthetic boughs of simulated trees.

"Look Mummy, look!" a happy little girl shouted with joy. "Goldilocks. And the Three Bears, Mummy."

Other children spied the costumed quartet and ran to them amid shouts of surprise and gleeful laughter.

"Let's take a picture!"

"Now hold hands with Goldilocks, dear!"

"Isn't that Baby Bear the cutest little thing!"

Goldilocks and the Three Bears danced and skipped and posed for family pictures. Hundreds of the happy tourists gathered around, smiling and applauding as the executioners played games with the children.

11

Liam O'Toole almost stopped in total disbelief when the terrorist vanished into thin air over the side of the balcony. Something—perhaps his own youthful experience with the gunmen of the Irish Republican Army—told him that kamikaze crazies didn't give up that easily.

He rushed outside, grabbing the steel railing to look down. There was no body—neither falling nor fallen. Not even a grease spot. Just thousands of college kids gathering for an open-air rock concert.

Momentarily perplexed, he caught movement in his right peripheral vision and turned. The terrorist hadn't jumped over; he'd jumped across. He stood on the adjacent balcony several feet away, desperately pulling on the door to a hotel room.

It was locked. He looked up in time to see the red-haired Irish merc spot him. O'Toole leaped for the edge of the balcony, and the terrorist fled. Scrambling onto the railing, he jumped to the next balcony.

With his pursuer closing in on him, the fugitive didn't wait to try the door. He ran to the end of the third balcony, climbed on top of the railing and jumped to the fourth.

The merc grabbed a window sill for support, climbed and propelled himself forward, landing on his feet on the concrete floor while the terrorist hurtled across the space to the next balcony. Just as O'Toole landed, the door to the hotel room opened and a top-less coed in skimpy panties looked at him in amazement. The Irishman's mouth dropped open.

"Later, babe." He rushed for the end of the balcony.

"Oh Bobbi!" the coed shrieked with delight to someone inside the room with her. "They're balcony hopping again!"

O'Toole ran past her, hurling himself over the three-foot space to the next balcony as the terrorist progressed to the fifth.

Bobbi, a twenty-two year old sophomore from Kentucky, staggered outside in his underwear. A can of beer hung loosely in his hand. Breakfast.

"Awright, radical to the max! Hey guys," he shouted into the hotel room, "follow me." He lurched to the end of the balcony in hot pursuit.

O'Toole hopped again, increasingly aware of the toll of his exertion and of the nine-story drop he faced if he ran out of steam on one of those three-foot gaps. But the distance was closing. The escaping terrorist had one more balcony to go, and that was it—corner of the building.

"Hey you! I wanna talk with you!" Liam shouted, climbing onto the railing to leap again. The terrorist was one balcony away. Suddenly Liam was aware of a thunderous roar below. He looked down. Thousands of people had turned from the sight of the open-air concert to the spectacle unfolding across the face of the hotel.

"Hey friend! I'm coming!" someone called to the merc in a mildly slurred voice. He turned in time to see Bobbi jump happily and land on his balcony.

From below came a roar of applause. Bobbi raised his arms like a big hero. Two balconies back, two of his friends poured from the hotel room and prepared to better—or at least meet—the Kentucky boy's challenge. Down below, excited photographers rushed back and forth in front of the hotel, yelling, "Go! Go! Jump! Come on, let's see it!"

Madness.

O'Toole saw the terrorist was about to jump for the last balcony, but when O'Toole leaped toward the balcony that was between them, the killer unexpectedly turned. The terrorist rushed him, his arms out, pushing O'Toole away from the railing before he landed.

CLAUDE HAYES found himself locked in arm-to-arm combat with the swarthy muscular man, who was OD'ing on the adrenaline of his fanaticism. Hayes's gun was knocked to the floor as the terrorist grabbed the black merc's neck, digging sharp bony thumbs deep into his throat.

Hayes choked. He closed his powerful hands around the terrorist's wrists, and tried to pull them away. The terrorist's hands were locked around Hayes's trachea like hydraulic wrenches. Hayes felt his lungs collapsing, grabbed the terrorist's head in one hand, his neck in the other and began twisting in opposite directions. The assassin let go, wriggling from

the merc's grip. Hayes gulped air. The terrorist
jumped for the detonator. Hayes kicked, the steel toe
of his boot catching the terrorist in the soft part under the chin. The man slammed backward, shrieking
with agony as his jaw slapped to one side. The fever-
ish intensity of martyrdom was gone from his eyes,
replaced by fear and desperation.

He flung himself at Hayes like a cornered rat, roar-
ing, his upper teeth bared. The lower part of his face
swung at an odd angle. His hands grappled for the
merc's eyes, digging in to gouge them out while his
teeth sank into Hayes's neck.

The merc recoiled from the disgusting sensation of
the mouth of the carnivorous rodent. Blindly he
grabbed the killer by the crown of his head and his
neck and ground his vertebrae together, pulverizing
the fragile spinal bones. The terrorist fell away from
the merc, his upper torso limp. With the last frenzied
attempt of the living organism to survive, he curled his
knee, slamming it between Hayes's legs.

The merc groaned as the pain thudded upward
through his groin, and he tossed the terrorist away
from him as if he were a terrible insect.

The assassin landed limply against a wall, still alive,
staring at Hayes with a blind, passionate need to kill.
His eyes laughed at the merc.

Hayes's eyes dropped toward the electric detonator
lying on the floor near the crates of mortars. The
dying terrorist tipped from the wall and collapsed
upon it. Murder was his final act.

O'TOOLE TWISTED FOR THE SIDE of the railing, away
from the terrorist's outstretched arms, but the move-

ment lost him momentum. He crashed against the balcony, lost his balance and fell. At the last moment he was barely able to grab the horizontal bar that ran along the bottom of the steel railing.

Nine stories below, the multitudes heaved a thunderous sigh of relief. Traffic in the street had come to a halt, and the boardwalk was jammed solid with spectators. Thousands more continued to pour from the beaches.

"Don't freak out man! I'm coming!" Bobby, the Kentucky sophomore, shouted, preparing to jump to O'Toole's rescue from the other balcony. One of his friends was right behind him and the third was making a leap. The topless girlfriend shouted her encouragement. She threw her arms wildly into the air, realized she was half-naked and hastily covered her breasts. The third guy made the leap. Again she forgot herself in her excitement and threw her arms wide.

Meanwhile, the terrorist came back, laughing and snarling. He tried to unhook O'Toole's fingers from the railing.

Thinking the man a rescuer, thousands of college kids watching below let out a mighty cheer.

"I'm coming!" Bobbi stood on the railing of the adjacent balcony and swung his arms back for the great leap. The terrorist gave up and ran to the end to make another jump. The spectators nine stories below booed and hissed. O'Toole saw his last chance. Gripping the iron struts of the railing tightly with his fists, he clenched his teeth and began to pull himself up.

Bobbi jumped.

The kooky college kid underestimated by about a foot and came down between balconies, reaching madly for something to hang on to. The closest thing was O'Toole's windbreaker.

The full weight of the hundred-and-sixty-pound student crashed down on the Irish merc's back. His hands were almost jerked away from the railing. He gripped tighter as the force of the sophomore's fall pulled him downward. The square edges of the steel bar sliced open the palms of his hands.

Bobbi shrieked with fear.

"Let go!" one of the photographers below yelled.

The crowd hissed and booed.

"Holy shit, Bobbi!" The other balcony-hopping students looked on uselessly from the adjacent deck. The terrorist reached the last balcony and pounded on the window.

Bobbi locked his arms around O'Toole's waist, twisting and spinning in panic while his legs kicked and dangled in midair. O'Toole sweated. He felt his hold weaken with every jolt from the hysterical man hanging on to him for dear life.

It's either you or me, O'Toole thought, feeling the young man slip farther down his chest. But Bobbi had one last chance. The Irish merc strained with the muscles of his lower back to push his legs and the dangling youth outward. He felt the student's grip weakening quickly. O'Toole moved his legs forward like a pendulum, gathering just enough momentum to swing Bobby forward at the moment the crazy college kid let go.

The Kentucky show-off was neatly deposited in a gasping terrified heap on the floor of the balcony below.

O'Toole winced and, for the second time, painfully began to draw himself up. Suddenly the entire building seemed to tremble in his hands. One corner of the ninth floor exploded outward in a shower of brick and glass.

CLAUDE HAYES DIVED from the room like a comet and the explosion hurled him even farther. The cinderblock wall in the corridor protected him from the full force of the blast but only for a moment. He rolled to his feet as a mortar blew haphazardly through the wall, exploding in an adjacent suite.

Room nine thirty-eight was a munitions warehouse ripe to blow. Pandemonium broke out as hotel guests ran from their rooms. Some shouted orders; others yelled hysterically. All ran for the exits. Smaller explosions reverberated through the building as mortars inside the end room blew in disordered sequence.

Hayes ran to the first open door as a tearful woman rushed out. "A man," she sobbed, pointing into her room. "Hanging on." She walked in a daze toward the fire exit. Hayes dashed inside and ran to the balcony. O'Toole was two balconies over.

There was bedlam on the Daytona Beach boardwalk as thousands of panicked college kids fled from the exploding missiles, trampling each other in their rush. The noise of the explosions mingled with screams from below. Mortars shot from the corner of the hotel, their smoky plumes arcing across the hot blue sky. Many shot harmlessly over the ocean. Others killed when they pounded into the beach or exploded over the heads of the fleeing crowd.

O'Toole was still clinging to the edge of the railing, his attempts to climb futile.

"Hang on buddy! I'm coming!" Hayes shouted.

He ran two doors down the corridor. The door was open and the room was deserted. A moment later he was on the balcony.

Against his will, Liam felt his fingers slowly open. Hayes reached through the bars and wrapped his powerful hand around the Irishman's wrist just as he let go.

Raising his arm, he lifted O'Toole steadily to the top of the railing, leaning to grab his belt and haul him over. The merc fell against the window, exhausted but thankful to be alive.

"Did you get the guy?" Hayes asked.

O'Toole gasped, still breathless, and pointed to the broken window of the room next door. Explosions continued to shake the building. Mortar ammunition blew through the walls and windows of the corner room, sailing in erratic trajectories over the fleeing crowds.

"He got away?"

"Not if I can help it," the red-haired Irishman said, gulping back big chestfuls of air and staggering toward the corridor. "The Trans Am. Come on! Let's take the stairs."

ALMOST IMMEDIATELY, police reports regarding late model yellow Chryslers began to come in as Barrabas and the mercs skimmed over the roofs and freeways of Orlando in the helicopter. None of the driver descriptions matched up until almost twenty minutes later, when a state trooper spotted a car driving erratically on Highway 4, southwest of Orlando.

"Keep the driver in sight," the mercenary leader transmitted through central police radio operators. "And report his progress until we're able to track from up here."

The chopper quickly left the sprawling urban mass behind, flying over swampland, tiny blue lakes and thousands of acres of citrus groves. Lined by slablike modern hotels and tourist centers, Highway 4 cut a swath westward through the countryside.

"In this part of Florida, all roads lead to Wonderworld," Major Carter shouted to Barrabas over the noise of the engines and the rotor.

The mercenary leader squinted to the west, where sunlight flowed like mercury over the turrets and domes of the fantasy playground. The high mock towers of Dracula's castle loomed above the greenery of forest and parks and the little lakes that dotted the giant tourist site. Rides and Ferris wheels glinted among the sparkling pavilions. The entire panoply of delights appeared fun and inviting under the searing sun and the deep blue Florida sky.

"There it is, Colonel!" Lee Hatton handed the field glasses to Barrabas in the front seat. The getaway car was changing into the right lane a half mile ahead of the chopper, angling through heavy traffic and moving onto a freeway exit. Simultaneously another police report confirmed that the suspect was on the exit ramp for Wonderworld.

Barrabas spoke clearly and carefully into the radio. "Put the Wonderworld security staff on full alert and inform them that we may be coming in by helicopter. But no one, I repeat, no one is to make any attempt to stop the car or the fugitive until further word from me. Over and out.''

"I guess this time, Johnny Burton has his hands full," Hatton commented as Barrabas signed off.

"We'll tail the car from a distance and go down once he gets through the main gates," he told Carter and the two mercs.

The vast thousand-acre complex was below them now, spread out like an eccentric city where half a dozen epochs and geographic regions had haphazardly fallen together. Oceans of parked cars spread across acres of tar. Thousands of visitors streamed toward a ferry boat and a monorail that carried them across a lake to Wonderworld's Enchanted Kingdom.

The Delta Force pilot kept the chopper hovering half a mile to the east of the parking lots while Barrabas trained the field glasses on the yellow Chrysler. Attendants in neat orange pantsuits waved the car into a space, and a short stocky man in tan fatigues emerged. He leaned back inside, slipped something in his jacket and carefully zipped it up despite the growing heat. Then he joined the rivers of tourists flowing toward the shores of the little blue lake. A long steel bullet train streaked across the water on a thin concrete filament, carrying passengers to the passenger area. The terrorist fell into the huge swarms moving onto the waiting ramps.

"Quick," Barrabas said to Carter, "Follow the monorail to the Enchanted Kingdom. Lee, Billy Two, we'll put you down inside the main gates. I want you to tail him on land from there. I'll scout from up here. We'll stay in contact with the walkie-talkies.''

"That should create quite a sensation," Lee muttered. She leaned over her MAC-10, checking to make sure the mag was fresh. "An armed military force landing in the middle of Wonderworld."

"Keep your weapons inside your jackets until you have to use them," Barrabas instructed. He had replaced his Sterling SMG with a MAC-10. The guns were compact enough to be relatively unobtrusive.

"We are invisible," said Billy Two. His unseen friend, Hawk Spirit, often told the Osage he was invisible in battle. Fine for Hawk Spirit. Bullets only went for flesh and blood.

Lee rolled her eyes.

The Indian nonchalantly tied a red bandanna around his forehead.

Below, Wonderworld, pleasure palace to the public of the most powerful nation of the world, beckoned. Jungle-like foliage grew along a winding miniature white-water river in Action Land while a roller coaster spiralled around the synthetic cowboy mesas of Pioneer Land. Future Land's exotic crinkled aluminum domes glittered in the yellow sunlight. The spiked turrets of Dracula's spooky castle towered over the Black Forest in Dream Land while throughout the parks and gardens, fairy-tale characters come-to-life frolicked with hordes of happy families.

The chopper banked over the lake, where dozens of tiny two-seater motorboats spun about, their occupants electric with happiness.

"Over there, behind those trees," Barrabas said, pointing. A miniature jungle separated Action Land from snack bars inside the main gates. Grass-covered slopes cleverly concealed a service area.

Throngs of curious people gathered for the show as Carter brought the chopper down slowly toward the lawns. He maintained a hover several feet above the ground. Hatton leaped from the side door and landed in a crouch, slipping momentarily. The grass was wet from an early-morning sprinkling. Hundreds had gathered at the perimeter of the slope, the children clapping and cheering with delight. But here and there, some faces registered doubt. The front of the crowd backed up and there was evident confusion about whether the landing was real or not. The crowd might turn at any moment, trampling one another in their panic to get away.

Billy Two landed and ran beside Lee from the wind stream as the helicopter spun up and away. Suddenly the Osage slipped in the wet grass. His legs slid out from under him, and he fell flat on his butt. His submachine popped out from the top of his jacket and slithered down the hill toward the crowd.

A woman shrieked, "My God, he's got a gun!" And the crowd drew back like ebbing on a beach. Still torn by their inability to distinguish fantasy from reality, the sightseers were on the verge of a major panic. And it would take only one person to set it off.

Billy Two somersaulted backward to his feet and promptly cartwheeled twice down the slope, grabbing his gun as he came up for the second time. He stood before the spectators, smiling proudly and throwing his arms into the air to beckon for applause.

The spell of fear was broken. The crowd whistled and cheered. Billy gave them an encore, jumping into a hostile posture with the gun in a ready-fire position. He ran along the front of the crowd making machine gun noises with his tongue. "Smile and wave good-bye," Starfoot muttered to the surprised Lee Hatton as he passed. Lee threw her fists up and cheered mightily for the Indian warrior.

Again, the Wonderworld visitors applauded. Parents armed with cameras rushed forward, children in tow.

Billy grabbed Lee's elbow and pulled her away from the surging crowd. He shouted, "Spectacular show in ten minutes. We come right back. Wait here for it."

Disappointed, the tourists groaned and fell back.

Billy Two slipped the gun back in his jacket as he and his partner broke into a run.

"See, I told you we were invisible."

"In a strange way, yeah. Landing right here in Action Land."

"Lee, Hawk Spirit says invisibility is always relative."

The mercs blended into the crowds flowing from Action Land. Signs pointed to The Avenue, the main street of a small town taken right out of white-picket-fence America. They followed it back to the main gates, where a field of brightly colored poppies welcomed newly arriving visitors to the land of sweet dreams. A group of blond cheerleaders led by a tanned, smiling, All-American type was siss-boom-bahing in the middle of the square.

"Look! There!" Billy Two spotted their man flashing some kind of identity card as he passed through a turnstile. The overhead sign was clearly marked Employees Only. The terrorist walked hastily into the strolling crowds on The Avenue.

"Keep an eye on him," said Lee. "I have a question for the attendant at the gate." She quickly made her way across the concourse. The elderly attendant wore a white suit with baby-blue piping.

"That man who just came through, he work here?" she asked.

"Sure does. Who's asking?"

"Oh, I work over in, uh, I'm a supervisor in Future Land and I haven't seen him around before."

"Well, that's because he works in Dream Land."

"Dream Land?"

"Yep. He's one of those actor types. Dresses up like a swan and runs around being silly. 'Bout as good a way of making money as being a politician, I suppose. Why I remember back in . . ."

The ticket taker's answer was another piece of the puzzle, but a crucial one, the single piece necessary to rough out a picture of the conspiracy. The idea was suddenly so terrible that Hatton shivered.

She excused herself and ran toward The Avenue. Billy Two's six-foot-six bearlike figure was clearly visible as he trailed the terrorist in the carefree ambling crowd. Hatton slipped the walkie-talkie from her pocket and turned it on.

She had to hurry. The nightmare was about to happen in Dream Land.

BARELY HAD THE HELICOPTER dropped the mercs and lifted out of Action Land when Nate came on the radio with an urgent message from Jessup.

"A bear costume!" Barrabas exclaimed, suddenly mystified. Instantly a picture of a gun hidden under a bulky suit formed in his mind's eye. It would be San Ysidro all over again. But this time it wouldn't be just one nut shooting up a crowd in a Fast Food restaurant. No, this time it would be death times a hundred. "I got it, Nate."

"I'm on the line with Wonderworld and the police now. We're electronically scanning the lists of recently hired employees but . . . "

"Well do it fast, Nate, while we still need it. Over and out."

"You heard that?" Barrabas clicked off the transmitter and looked at Carter.

The pilot nodded. "Pick a spot," he said doubtfully, gesturing with his chin at the sprawling theme park below.

"Bears. Where in hell would bears . . ." He needed more to go on. Was he looking for a man dressed as a grizzly bear in Pioneer Land? Or Smoky the Bear in Action Land? One bear or any number of terrorists in a variety of perfect disguises. There could be dozens of the sick vermin. There was no way of knowing until it was too late.

His walkie-talkie beeped, and he flicked it on. It was Lee.

"We're following north on The Avenue and the target is heading straight for Dracula's castle. Colonel, the man came through the employee's gate and apparently works as an animal actor in Dream Land. I have a hunch he's on his way there now."

"Lee, information via Walker Jessup confirms your hunch. Don't let him out of your sight, and watch anyone, repeat anyone, wearing a costume. Over and out." He turned to the pilot. "Let's go to Dream Land."

"ISN'T THAT THE CUTEST BABY BEAR!" a mother baby-talked to her big-eyed little girl. The Three Bears mocked horror at the sight of Goldilocks and pretended to flee by running in circles around her.

The mesmerized little girl was one of hundreds strolling under "gas" streetlamps in the cobblestone square where the gabled houses of eighteenth-century London had been perfectly reproduced. The fact that the buildings were constructed to two-thirds scale lent an air of quaint coziness to Dream Land.

The other side of the square fronted on the Magic Forest. The Gingerbread House poked its gables through the treetops, and Hansel and Gretel danced around the oven with the wicked witch. Humpty-Dumpty teetered on a wall, with young men in beef-eater's costumes playing all the king's men. A giant cat played the fiddle near the old-fashioned facade fronting the entrance to the cable car station. And overhead, brightly colored cars floated on their slender cable, going past the towers of Dracula's ominous castle toward the glittering domes of Future Land. Elran saw this from a distance, his field of vision restricted by the eye holes in the steel-headed bear costume. He bobbed as he played with the visitors, gauging the numbers entering the square. The big crowds were in the morning. Jason the cheerleader and his band of blondes leaped into view and jumped across the cobblestones, tossing their batons in time to the omnipresent polka music. It was time.

"Howard! Come on Howard. Brittany and Lance want their pictures taken with the bears!" A fleshy woman in a deep turquoise pantsuit flagged her husband over and pushed her two children toward the Three Bears. A helicopter zipped around the side of Dracula's castle.

"Now smile, children."

Baby Bear took his work very seriously indeed. He turned to Momma and Poppa Bear and nodded once. His great paw slid into the furry folds of his costume and grasped the zipper.

"No, Lance! Move closer to Brittany. That's right."

"Wonderworld! Wonderworld! Rah! Rah! Rah!"

The woman in turquoise snapped the picture, and Goldilocks danced farther into the crowd.

"Now us! Now us!" Another family ran to line up beside the Three Bears. Elran pulled the zipper down and reached inside his suit. The crowd parted on one side, and Hammer, the leader of the missing cell, appeared. His hand went inside his jacket. Suddenly the air vibrated from the noisy whop-whop of a helicopter rotor. A shadow, like that of a great predatory bird, fell upon Dream Land.

There was a disturbance at the back of the crowd of spectators.

"All right, now! All the animals! Come on over here. Little Bo Peep, Humpty-Dumpty!" Jason and his cheerleaders jumped in front of the Three Bears. "Everyone together in the 'Royal—"

When Baby Bear pulled a dangerous-looking weapon from inside his costume, the enthusiatic actor's first thought was that he had missed a rehearsal. He didn't remember this part at all. It was a sudden challenge to his professionalism. Momma and Poppa Bear suddenly had guns, too. Think quick, Jason told himself. Ad-lib something—fast!

Someone nearby started screaming.

The gun was pointed right at Jason.

Baby Bear fired.

12

"Now we wait," Nate said to Walker Jessup, swiveling away from the computer console. In Daytona and Orlando, Barrabas and the SOBs had moved. Several minutes earlier, the first reports from the Coast Guard and navy ships searching for Nanos and Bishop had come in. They had discovered wreckage, but no trace of the missing mercs.

"I just can't believe it," the Fixer said, heaving his big body up from a chair and pacing awkwardly. "They were too good. Both of them. I can't believe that someone took them both out. Can you? I mean, they'd back each other up, wouldn't they?"

Nate Beck looked down.

"Yeah. Yeah, sure they would," he said uncomfortably. But at the back of his mind was a lingering doubt. Bishop and Nanos had never been friends. What if one of them hadn't reacted fast enough. What if... He couldn't even bring himself to think about it.

All the mercs knew the ultimate price that was sometimes paid. Many of their buddies and best friends had already bought it—in an Iranian desert, on a ship off the coast of Central America, in a siege in the countryside of Majorca. But not Alex Nanos, the guy who loved women and parties and good times, wild times. Not Geoff Bishop, the quiet Canadian. This was going to hurt all of them in a way they were unprepared for. And although he knew Lee Hatton would accept it bravely and without any open display of sorrow, it was going to hurt her especially. Death did strange things to the living. He hoped she wouldn't somehow feel responsible.

Jessup banged the desk with his fist as hard as he could. "Damn!" he said, wincing. "I don't believe. No, I don't believe it."

He reached for the telephone.

"Jessup.... Yes, Walker Jessup. How many other Jessups have you been talking to on this line?... Your apology is accepted. I want a chopper up here on the roof immediately.... No, it's not for a commando operation. I want to track some of the search ships.... Captain, if it's not up here in two minutes or less picture seeing Alaska with your ass in a sling."

The burly Texan slammed the receiver down.

"You have to be here?" he asked Nate.

The computer expert nodded. "In case something comes through. And the colonel asked me to check on a few miscellaneous things when the pace slowed. I should do it now."

"They're out there somewhere, Nate. I know it. I feel it in my gut. They have to be."

Jessup ambled slowly to the roof-top landing pad, without looking back. A deep fatigue was creeping slowly over him after the long relentless night. His thick shoulders drooped heavily, but his spirit, though weighted by sadness, refused to acknowledge the almost certain fate of two lost men.

BY THE TIME Hayes and O'Toole ran from the hotel, Daytona Beach was awash with screams of panic and sirens. An occasional mortar still exploded, blowing chunks of brick and cinderblock from the ninth-floor corner of the hotel. Smoky plumes trailed across the sky. Most of the mortars had gone over the heads of the sunbathers and concert fans, exploding harmlessly in the surf. But others had impacted on the beach, leaving a cratered battlezone littered with burning cars and dead people.

The great multitude of students had fled out of range to the end of the boardwalk, half a mile away. A giant traffic jam had spread across the southern end of the beach. Flames from the combat zone spread, and exploding gas tanks punctuated the howl of ambulances and fire trucks. Hundreds tried desperately to drive their cars to safety. Souped-up Camaros and fancy Fieros spun their wheels and sank to their axles in sand.

"There!" Hayes shouted, pointing over the heads of the people who had gathered on the street outside the front of the hotel. The short, wiry man with the handlebar moustache was making his way rapidly along the sidewalk that ran past the back doors of the amusement arcades and the miniature-golf courses.

"I got it! I got it!" The bearded New York photographer ran in circles, salivating and holding his camera like a trophy. "I got a picture of it!"

"What do you figure he's going to do?" O'Toole asked as the two mercs pushed into the crowd.

"The car is loaded with explosives. He drives it into the thick of those cars trying to leave the beach and sets it off."

"Right. No one can move because they're all stuck. Anyone who misses death in the initial explosion is burned alive in a ring of fire."

The sidewalk was suddenly clear of people, and the terrorist walked briskly, craning his neck to look between buildings and amusement park rides at the beach. The two mercs reached inside their jackets to rest their hands on their guns.

The terrorist looked over his shoulder, his eyes crossing O'Toole's with the sudden shock of recognition.

"He's spotted us," O'Toole said, pulling his gun out and breaking into a run.

The assassin pulled a handgun from his jacket and fired twice, forcing O'Toole to dive into the street. The assassin looked about quickly and darted through the back door of an amusement arcade.

The mercs tore after him, thudding down a short flight of stairs. The front of the long narrow arcade opened onto the boardwalk. It was empty, the games and rides having been deserted when the occupants fled from the nearby explosions. The mercs carefully surveyed the shadows under the giant faces of smiling clowns on a carousel, behind the twisting metal arms of the Spider, beneath the rows of video and pinball games, behind the Tilt-a-Whirl, near the miniature Ferris wheel that revolved mindlessly amid the silence of flickering lights.

"Let's try to get him alive," Hayes said, moving rapidly to the front while O'Toole covered.

Suddenly the terrorist was there, squeezed beside the seat on the floor of one of the Tilt-a-Whirl cars. He fired as the car spun past the merc. Bullets slammed into the row of pinball machines. The bells and buzzers went nuts, setting off a crazy chorus of rings and beeps. The Tilt-a-Whirl kept turning, spinning the killer out of sight.

A loud explosion from a mortor reverberated through the arcade. Shrill cries and shouts rose again, followed by the rapid explosions of gas tanks. Fanned by ocean winds, the fire was sweeping along the roofs of the cars. Hundreds abandoned their cars and fled toward the boardwalk. Someone had sideswiped the red Trans Am in their flight to safety, and now the bomb-laden car was tangled amid a dozen other cars that had been abandoned to fate. Obscured by the thick black clouds from burning rubber and plastics, the long orange flames greedily licked toward the boardwalk and pier.

O'Toole peered from behind the cover of the pinball machines as the midway ride came around again. The Tilt-a-Whirl car whirled and tilted. A row of video game screens blew into pieces as the terrorist loosed another round, driving the merc back behind the pinball game. The terrorist jumped from the Tilt-a-Whirl and bolted for the steps leading back to the street. The soldiers of Barrabas raced after him, bounding up the stairs and crouching when they reached the street level. The terrorist had disappeared. O'Toole turned in time to see him dash up some steps to the roof of the arcade, where the miniature-golf course had been set among giant pink elephants and friendly dinosaurs. O'Toole hit Hayes, running. "There he is."

The Trans Am blew into a thousand fragments, the deadly metal splinters hurtling like shrapnel. Mounds of incendiary material flew upward and dropped over a wide radius, raining on the heads of the people who had retreated to the other side of the pier. Human torches shrieked and ran mindlessly down the beach to the ocean. Thousands of college kids, twice panicked, fled, pushing over one another in a feral frenzy of escape.

Hayes grabbed O'Toole and pulled him into the shelter of a miniature lighthouse as burning cinders and sharp metal debris hailed down. Fire caught at the lacquered wood dinosaur and the pink elephant, almost instantly transforming them into giant torches.

The terrorist leaped to the top of the wall at the end of the roof and looked down. Hordes of panicked people swept down the asphalt strip like floodwater from a bursting dam. He was trapped. His mission was completed. He turned, waving the automatic pistol in front of him.

The mercs moved out from the lighthouse as flames began to spread across the tar on the roof. The terrorist fired.

O'Toole dropped to his knee and calmly fired a three-round burst from his MAC-10 submachine gun. Three red spots opened up on a diagonal across the killer's chest. He teetered on the wall, concentrating his last remaining strength on his gun, trying to raise it and fire again.

O'Toole and Hayes moved quickly across the roof toward him, watching carefully.

The terrorist retreated from them, tipping over the edge of the wall. He flung his arms out, desperately trying to regain his balance. A shriek of terror escaped his lips as he fell backward, headfirst into the onrushing crowd.

Hayes and O'Toole looked down.

The terrorist sank beneath the feet of the stamped-ing herd like a stone in water. In their mad confusion, the panicked vacationers scarcely noticed the fallen body. The terrorist heard thunder. The vacationers kept going. His arms appeared briefly as he made a last desperate attempt to claw his way up to the light. The force the terrorist had unleashed was self-preservation. It crushed him, ground him underfoot to little more than bloody pulp.

LEE HATTON AND BILLY TWO kept the terrorist in sight as they passed into the crowds under the arches of Dracula's castle.

"Keeping your boots on this time?" Lee mur-mured to the Osage.

"Damn betcha," he growled. "When these people begin to run, many toes will be stepped on."

"Why don't you ask Hawk Spirit to do something about that?"

"Hawk Spirit say you and I are invulnerable."

"That wasn't exactly what I meant."

A group of cheerleaders burst past them as they crossed a wide drawbridge and emerged in a cobble-stoned square surrounded by ersatz Tudor houses. A sign announced they were in Dream Land and pointed to the Magic Forest. Peter Rabbit hopped by, leading a herd of laughing children toward a group of jug-glers. Everywhere, thrilled visitors to Wonderworld capered hand in hand with furry friends. The mercs worked the crowd with their eyes, dreading the mo-ment when, without warning, clowns would become killers.

The terrorist plunged ahead, moving after the cheerleaders into a gathering at the entrance to the Magic Forest. He started to unzip his jacket as he jostled through.

Lee raised the walkie-talkie as the shadow of the chopper fell over the crowd.

"Colonel, he's going to—"

"I can see him, Lee," their commander's words came back, terse and clear. "Go for it!"

As the killer came to the front of the crowd, Billy Two saw him reach inside his jacket.

"Stop!" The massive Indian threw himself into the surprised visitors, shoving them aside.

"Hey, whaddaya think you're trying to pull," asked a responsible father, moving into Billy Two's path and raising his arms belligerently. The Osage swatted him out of the way.

Lee jumped through the opening.

"Stop!" Billy Two commanded.

A woman screamed.

"Oh my God, my God, my God!"

Great red holes blew open across the back of Jason's T-shirt. People in the front row raised their hands to block the splashing gore. The blond cheerleaders abandoned their batons in midair and fled, screaming.

Lee Hatton pulled her MAC-10 to her hip. Her teeth ground together as she squeezed on the trigger, mowing a line of retaliation toward the gunman in the Baby Bear outfit. Synthetic fur flew as big holes opened up across his chest. From the corner of her eye, she watched Goldilocks slide into the crowd. Lee was only vaguely aware of noise, shouts, madness and the flurry of movement around her. She was totally aware of the submachine guns in the hands of the other two bears.

She aimed to the right, and Mr. Bear suddenly did a jerking dance, dropping his automatic weapon. The bullets spun him backward with resounding force, slamming him against a thick tree. He went into permanent hibernation.

Meanwhile, Baby Bear was sliding out of sight. Starfoot turned his submachine gun toward him. Bullets pounded across the costume animal's back and opened a swath in the fur of his head. Twice invulnerable to the lead death, Baby Bear kept moving. Impossible, thought Billy Two. Hawk Spirit wouldn't do that.

Momma Bear's gun barked and bullets whined past Billy Two's elbow. He yelped as a searing line burned across the skin of his arm. His jacket sleeve smiled bloodily below his shoulder.

Hawk Spirit *did* do that. Old unreliable. He'd answer for this—to Billy Two. The Osage ignored the pain. He snarled like a grizzly and cut open across Lee's line of fire. Mrs. Bear's oversized furry head blew open, and the terrorist's forehead lifted off her face in an explosion of blood. Behind the two mercs, Hammer opened up on the panicking crowd, loosing a mag into the backs of fleeing tourists. Mothers and fathers shrieked, children screamed, baby carriages and strollers plowed into slow-moving senior citizens, knocking them aside. Children stood frozen in terror or ran yelping hysterically toward shrubbery. A fat man tried to jump into a litter can. Hammer picked him off.

People fell, sudden streams of blood jetting from heads and guts. Sometimes they moaned in terrible pain and writhed on the cobblestones. Others dropped, quivered briefly in final death spasms and were still. Seeing an opportunity to slow his prey, Hammer lowered the barrel of his submachine gun to shoot their legs out from under them. The fleeing stumbled over the bodies of the fallen, and those rushing behind them stepped on the ones who were down. Shrieks of pain and terror ripped through Dream Land as the young, the clumsy and the very old were trampled.

Billy Two twirled around, sending a withering wind of bullets at the cold-blooded assassin, dismembering him with the full force of the 32-round magazine.

The rampaging mob of panic-stricken tourists rode the wind of their screams, flying for safety toward Dracula's castle or into the boutiques in the quaint gabled houses. Lee Hatton spotted Goldilocks twenty feet away at the edge of the fleeing crowd. She was rummaging in her basket of flowers at the door of a snack bar disguised as an old English tavern.

She didn't look scared. She looked determined.

Hatton ran toward her, holding her MAC like a pistol. "Stop!" she cried.

Goldilocks looked up, pulling a square package from a tangle of straw flowers in her basket. She raised her arm to throw it. Lee fired. The lead double punched. The terrorist's long wig of golden hair sailed off as her guts opened. The force of the bullets socked her backward into the tavern-snack bar. The old-fashioned doors swung shut. Then they exploded outward, the shock waves bowling Hatton over. The windows of Dream Land broke, and glass cascaded from in the upper floors of the recreated eighteenth-century buildings. A wave of flame suddenly licked upward through the tavern, eating its way quickly into the adjacent houses. Three hundred years after the first one, the great fire of London had begun anew.

Billy Two and Hatton instantly regrouped. The woman's face was blackened from the explosion and cut by long scratches from her tumble on the cobblestones. Dream Land was still loud with hysterical screams, but the square was almost empty now. Bodies lay sprawled in bloody puddles across the once-idyllic streets. Some were dead, some moaning in pain. Thick dark smoke from burning plastics used in the construction of the ersatz village began to fill the air.

"There he is!" Lee shouted, seeing the third and last bear running quickly after the crowd, which was fleeing into the Magic Forest. Suddenly bullets skidded past them from behind. The two mercs hit the cobblestones, rolling away from the fire.

Wonderworld security guards were rushing across the drawbridge from Dracula's castle. Some wore blue uniforms. Others were in suits and wore dark glasses. Walkie-talkies hung from their belts. They held guns, and they were firing straight at Barrabas's soldiers.

BARRABAS WATCHED ELRAN ESCAPE through the madness that the terrorist had unleashed in the fantasy playground. He cut sideways at the back of the fleeing crowd and headed toward the cable car station. The people in line had rushed into the forest, and the attendants were quickly fleeing to the shelter of a service area, leaving the ride running automatically.

One by one the little colored cars left the station and, hanging from the steel cable stretching to Future Land, glided high over Dracula's castle. When the terrorist disappeared momentarily on the stairs that led to the platform, Barrabas knew the escape had been well thought out in advance. The cable car was the only way past the frenetic mob stampeding the exits from Dracula's castle and the Magic Forest. The terrorist was going to sail right over their heads.

Sirens reverberated across the tourist playground as state police drove through the gates and armed agents swarmed onto the grounds. The panic spread freely. Ten thousand people began a stampede from an enemy they did not know to a refuge they would not find.

"Colonel Barrabas!" the Delta Force pilot shouted. "Down at the drawbridge!"

Wonderworld's armed security staff rushed from the fake castle into Dream Land, firing at the first unauthorized people they saw who had guns. Hatton and Starfoot hit the ground and rolled away from the fire that had been mistakenly turned against them.

"Bank down and fly between!" Barrabas yelled, hanging on to straps by the window. Carter lowered the chopper so fast that Barrabas felt as if his seat had fallen out. The Delta major sank to within inches of the cobblestones and buzzed toward the security men at knee level. They hit the dirt, flat on their bellies. The helicopter careened away from the burning houses, flying through an acrid cloud of dense black smoke.

ACROSS THE COBBLESTONED SQUARE, the escaping terrorist climbed into a cable car, still wearing his protective bear suit. The blue pod with open sides left the platform and slid gracefully over the roof of the spooky castle. On the castle's other side, hordes of tourists fled with their children down The Avenue, making for the main gates.

Elran slammed a new mag into his gun. The cable car trip would give him a bird's-eye view and a deadly aiming position high above thousands of panicking people. And he had plenty of spare mags strapped inside the bear costume. He rested the barrel on the metal edge of the car and scanned for a target area that would give him maximum casualties.

Darkness fell over him. He saw the shadow of a helicopter growing larger on the ground below. The chopper was dropping from the sky—on top of him.

He turned in time to see orange muzzle fire from the barrel of a submachine gun held by a white-haired man riding in the cockpit beside the pilot. The bullets punched into him like iron fists, knocking the air from his lungs and throwing him to the floor of the cable car. He raised his gun, fighting to catch his breath. A single thought fired through him: after this terrible day, no American would ever again feel safe in his own country. The hideous massacre at Wonderworld would be one of terrorism's greatest victories.

He squeezed the trigger, and a line of punctures appeared across the roof on the helicopter, almost hitting the delicate rotor mechanism. The pilot flew upward and was blocked from Elran's view by the roof of the cable car. The loud noise of the engine was right overhead.

The terrorist pulled himself to his knees, still gasping for breath. The cable car was swinging back and forth. He pushed himself carefully to his feet, fighting to keep his balance. Not knowing from which direction the chopper would attack again, he twisted fearfully as the cable car passed over the high, peaked turrets of Dracula's castle.

There was a brief lull.

The noise from the helicopter was still directly overhead, but it seemed to be ebbing, as if the chopper was flying upward. Suddenly the sound of the rotor vibrated in the air around him. the cockpit dropped into view right beside the cable car. Nile Barrabas swung across the space feet first and landed beside Elran. The merc and terrorist were instantly locked tight in hand-to-hand combat high above Wonderworld. Barrabas deftly grabbed the man's gun hand, knocking it against the steel edge of the car. He slammed his fist under the hard steel chin of the bear costume. The terrorist yelped. Gun and bear head fell from the cable car onto Dracula's castle, where they slithered and rolled down the shingles, landing somewhere in the midst of the panic below. Barrabas looked into the glowing eyes of a maniac. Foam gathered at the corner of the terrorist's mouth.

The mercenary slammed his fists into Elran's stomach until the killer doubled over in pain. Then Barrabas rammed his knee upward, smashing Elran in the face.

The terrorist lost it. He collapsed against the side of the cable car, his body unable to respond. Gasping for breath, he looked up at the colonel, his bloodshot eyes bulging in fanatical hatred.

"We will come like flies upon you," he said hoarsely, blood spitting from his mouth. His hand slipped inside the bear suit.

"So come," Barrabas said, curling his lip. "In this state you'll get strapped into a chair and zapped with two thousand volts for what you did today." He reached down and grabbed Elran by the fur collar of his costume.

With a sudden burst of unsuspected energy, the terrorist's hand emerged from the bear suit, clenching one of the spare magazines. He bashed it into Barrabas's eyes, cutting a long gash across his forehead. Instantly blood poured over the colonel's face.

Kicking and scrambling, Elran pushed away from the colonel and sat on the side of the moving cable car. The roof of Dracula's castle, barely ten feet below, still offered him a last possibility of escape. He swung his legs over.

Barrabas, blinded by his own blood, grabbed for Elran, his hands closing around the back of the bulky bear costume just as the terrorist pushed off. The terrorist's weight jerked Barrabas to the open side of the car.

The murderous fugitive squawked, his legs dangling only a few feet above the top of the castle. It was almost too late. The pod continued to glide along the steel cable. In a few seconds the terrorist faced a drop of over a hundred feet and certain death. Turning his head against his shoulder to wipe the blood from his eyes, Barrabas held on as the man struggled.

Still clutching the magazine, Elran reached behind his neck and struck at the hands that held him back from his final jump to freedom.

Barrabas clenched his teeth against the pain and strained to pull the man into the car. The skin of his hands broke and blood ran between his fingers. The fabric of the bear suit was ripping. There was no way he was going to get the man back in the cable car.

He looked down into the whites of the fanatical eyes.

"You want down!" he shouted angrily.

Elran snarled like a rabid animal.

"So go down!" He leaned over the side of the cable car, bringing his face within inches of the terrorist's and spoke in a low voice filled with contempt. "And on the way down, mad dog, have a look at the slaughter of innocence."

Barrabas strained against the limits of his endurance to grip the terrorist just a moment longer. The last turret of the castle was underneath, its peaked roof tipped by a long steel lightning rod.

Terrorist time was up.

Barrabas timed it to the split second. He let go. Elran dropped like a stone directly onto the pointed castle turret. The lightning rod held. The bulletproof vest inside the bear costume didn't. The terrorist's mouth opened, emitting a roar of agony as the steel stake impaled him. He swung in the high winds like a furry brown beast on a spit, a macabre trophy of his own scheme of revenge, his dying eyes the final witness to the bloody carnage in Dream Land below.

13

It was daylight by the time Geoff Bishop pulled the rubber dinghy onto a deserted beach on Terra Ceia Bay. Alex Nanos drifted in and out of consciousness, at times delirious, at times staring silently at Bishop.

The Canadian merc carried Nanos up to the beach and set him on blankets in the shade of some Australian pines. The wounded merc was raging with fever. Both he and Bishop desperately needed water.

Alex was conscious now, but his hold on consciousness was so tenuous that he barely knew where he was, what was happening around him or how long it had been since he'd been hurt. Yet somehow the small part of him that remained lucid was aware of his former rival's Herculean efforts, and that he owed him his life. "Some job," Alex said hoarsely, his lips parched and cracked.

Bishop looked up, surprised. They were the first words Nanos had spoken to him since their boat was blown out of the water.

"I'm going to get help here as soon as I can, Alex. I have to leave you." Bishop covered the merc with a blanket.

Alex looked at his rescuer. There was something he wanted to say, but the thought seemed to dart away, hiding in the inner recesses of his mind.

"You'll be okay?" Bishop asked.

Nanos nodded, still trying to grab the fugitive thought. It was important, something he had to tell Bishop, but his concentration was too dissipated by fever and the loss of blood.

"I gotta take care of one of these scum bags. Someone else'll come for you, Alex. Soon. You'll be okay, won't you?"

Nanos grabbed Bishop suddenly by the collar of his windbreaker as the airman pulled away. He clung tightly but still the critical words escaped him.

Bishop gently pried the Greek's hand away. "I gotta go, Alex. It's life or death. I gotta go. You'll be okay. I'll send help to get you. Tell me you'll be okay. You won't go anywhere, you know...."

Alex relaxed, breathing deeply, aware of the urgency in the Canadian merc's voice. He still couldn't remember what he had to say.

"Get them, Geoff," he murmured, his words barely audible. "I'll be okay. You get them good."

"I will. And I'll see you in a while, buddy."

Nanos watch Bishop slip quickly into the forest along the shore. Just as Bishop disappeared among the bushes, it came to him. Nanos tried to pull himself up, anxious to say it before his rescuer was gone.

It was too late. Bishop faded from sight. Nanos's burst of energy quickly evaporated. He fell back on to the blanket, weak, dizzy and barely conscious. But he remembered. He knew what he had forgotten to say to

Bishop. It was important. He wanted to say, "Thanks."

Bishop faded into the bushes, wading through a brackish slough. Several hundred yards inland he came to a clearing near a sand pit where a packed gravel road ended. Garbage and old appliances had been thrown into the tall grass, and the air was rank with the smell of a dead animal.

For the first time, Bishop stood still and took stock of himself and his position. His body ached all over with a dull even pain that sank to the center of his bones. Much of his skin on one side had suffered first- and second-degree burns in the explosion. It was red, and in places blisters had broken out. His hair had been singed. His face and arms were streaked with cuts and scrapes. His feet were bare, and only the jacket he had found on the yacht covered his back. His pants were torn and wet and hung at his waist.

He looked half-dead, like some creature from the twisted imagination of a Hollywood horror-film writer. He had barely a couple of hours to stop the destruction on the Skyway Bridge, and in the meantime he had to convince someone he was legit. He was thirsty, hungry, exhausted and on the verge of collapse. He had made a decision to do whatever was necessary short of taking an innocent life to stop the madman with the bomb.

The gravel road led through a marsh and occasional patches of thick, jungle-like forest. Tire ruts from heavy vehicles had baked into the dry earth beside the narrow road, but there was little indication of recent use.

More than a mile later, the road ran across a field,and passed a dilapidated mobile home. An old man tinkered under the hood of an ancient '57 Chevy outside the screened porch.

Bishop watched for a few minutes. Then he crept along the road, taking cover behind bushes until he was able to walk up the driveway. The old man didn't notice the stranger until Bishop was behind him. The airman locked his arm around the man's neck in a half nelson.

"Shut up and nothing will happen," Bishop told him, as the old guy squirmed. "Is there anyone else here?"

The man shook his head. "Just me."

"Wilbert!" a woman called from inside the house.

"Let's go." Bishop pushed him toward the mobile home.

The old woman was sitting at a kitchen table, slicing strawberries with a paring knife. The bowl fell and smashed and the woman shrieked when Bishop pushed her husband in the door. He forced the old man into a chair. The woman looked at the man and burst into tears.

"Don't be frightened. Nothing's going to happen to you," he assured them. "I can't explain why this is necessary, but it is, and eventually you'll understand."

Confronted by the scarred, disheveled stranger who acted like a madman, the elderly couple remained immobile, frozen by fear and shock.

"You have a phone?"

The couple looked at each other, and the old man shook his head.

"The car work?"

The man nodded.

"Good."

Bishop ripped an extension cord from a wall socket and quickly bound their hands and legs, tying the cord loosely to avoid hurting them or cutting off their circulation. It wouldn't take them more than half an hour to worm their way out of the bonds. It was nine o'clock. All he needed was an hour. The old people had the living daylights scared out of them, but they were okay. Bishop saw the woman's purse on a table in the living room. He found her wallet, taking a handful of change and some one dollar bills. Then he went to the sink turned on the tap and sucked back a mouthful of cold water.

"Take anything, anything you want, just leave us be. I'll give you our money. We got five hundred dollars...."

"Wilbert," the woman said, sobbing again, "not our life's savings to that man...."

"I don't want your life's savings, lady, just a little bit of cash, and I'll pay you back. And I'm not going to hurt you. I need the car. And some time."

"Keys are in it," the old man said. "Just leave us be."

"How far is Highway 19?"

"'Nuther mile."

"In an hour I'll call the police and tell them to come get you. If they're not here by the time you get free yourselves, phone them and tell them there's a man on the beach at the end of the road. He's very badly hurt and needs medical attention. Tell them that. Promise me!"

The couple exchanged glances again, clearly puzzled by the stranger's odd behavior. In Florida, witnesses to crimes in isolated country spots were usually murdered.

"Why you doing this, son?"

"I can't explain," Bishop said, turning as he went through the screen door. "Just promise me."

The old man nodded reluctantly.

"You making a heap o' trouble for yourself, young man."

"It's the only way, old man."

"I don't believe that, son."

"Believe it."

The '57 Chevy purred like a kitten and drove like tiger, gliding over the dusty road. After a mile and a half he hit Highway 19, several hundred yards before the Skyway toll plaza.

Heavy morning traffic was lined up in front of the booths but moving quickly. Bishop dug out one of the dollar bills.

"Got the time?" he asked as he handed it to a uniformed woman as he drove through.

"Nine forty-five, mister. Here's your receipt." She looked him over casually when she gave him the slip of paper. He grabbed it and pulled through.

There was no sign of the silver Lincoln at the plaza. He stepped on the gas, merging into the traffic, with his eyes peeled for the rest area the man on the yacht had mentioned. The delicate concrete arch of the new Skyway came into view, sweeping high over the waters of Tampa Bay. Bright morning sunlight glinted on the webs of steel suspension cables reaching from the twin towers.

A tourist information sign advertised a rest stop, and he saw the parking area off the main highway. He turned on his right blinker to pull over, and his heart leaped. The silver Lincoln was near the entrance, merging into the traffic waiting to cross the newly opened bridge.

There was still time.

Soon the nightmare of endurance would finally be over.

HELICOPTERS HOVERED OVER the long slender arches of the Skyway Bridge, part of the elaborate security arrangements for the official opening. Traffic was still being diverted onto the old span, the rusting iron girders that the new two-hundred-million-dollar bridge was to replace. State trooper cars blocked the entrance to the new Skyway, which was lined with a dozen polished black limousines. From his seat beside the pilot in one of the overhead choppers, Walker Jessup watched the dignitaries and the press corps and photographers, who gathered at the height of the span as the official opening ceremonies got under way.

Through his field glasses, Jessup saw the governor step onto a portable platform to follow the mayors of St. Petersburg and Bradenton in their dedication speeches. No doubt the politicians were paying lip service to the innocent people who had died when the outer span of the old bridge had collapsed several years earlier.

It was an unjust and cruel irony that the real heroes of the land, Barrabas's soldiers, would never be commemorated in a similar way. He had just seen a few pieces of the scattered wreckage of the mercs' cruiser off the shores of Egmont Key. Coast Guard ships had already made positive identification. There was no sign of survivors.

Knowing loyal men who had died, who had disappeared into the emptiness of their own duty, was a scar that could never entirely heal.

Both Geoff Bishop and Alex Nanos, whatever the rivalries between them, had been popular with the other mercs. Their loss would be taken very hard. Barrabas would survive it. The Texan was sure of that. The hard-nosed warrior would retreat into silence for a time to mull it over, lick his wounds, accept it. But Jessup worried about how it would affect Lee Hatton. He worried that it might demoralize the mercs to the point where they were no longer the tight, highly effective unit of fighting men they were now.

Those were the risks. He was the one who had recruited Barrabas and had helped the veteran professional soldier put the covert action squad together. If it happened, if the team collapsed, then the Fixer would start over again. And he'd talk Barrabas into it, too. The world needed men and women like these if it was going to survive.

"Where to now?" the chopper pilot asked.

Jessup lowered the field glasses. The governor had finished his speech and snipped the ribbon across the road. The dignitaries headed for their limousines. At the entrance to the new span, state troopers pulled their cars away. A long line of traffic waited eagerly to cross the newly opened Skyway.

"Tampa," Walker Jessup said. "Back to the base."

THE FLORIDA GOVERNOR STOOD to one side of the newly opened bridge, conferring with his political aides on the news arriving from Daytona Beach and Orlando.

"Any estimates yet?" he asked, his face lined with concern.

"We're talking at least a hundred casualties," one said. "Millions in direct physical damages. Damage to the tourist industry will be impossible to calculate. And it's not over yet."

"What about this man Barrabas and his team. You say they're responsible for closing in on the terrorists?"

"Apparently, sir. Burton has clammed up in Orlando. We don't know yet if they've actually managed to save lives or if their actions have cost lives."

"If they have, I'll have Barrabas's head on a platter," the governor said.

"Bob," Roger Davies said moving to the governor's side and speaking softly, "we're running out of time. You were due off the bridge five minutes ago. The state troopers have let the first cars through already."

"Sir," the governor's press secretary interrupted, "the press corps just got word of what's happening in Orlando. They're not going to leave until you give them a statement."

The governor glanced at his old friend and mentor, then turned to the press secretary. "I'll speak to them...."

"Bob, you're on a tight schedule today," Davies said, the urgency unmistakable in his voice.

The governor looked at Davies, suddenly concerned. "Are you feeling all right, Roger? You're white."

"I'm fine, Bob. I'm just concerned about your schedule."

The Florida governor turned to the press secretary. "Tell the reporters I'll come over and make a brief statement just to say I don't know enough to make a statement. That should hold them for a while."

The press secretary quickly made her way to the reporters, who had gathered in a narrow service area near the center of the suspension span. The governor turned to Roger Davies and smiled.

"Usually you're telling me to take it easy and to hell with the schedule, Roger. What's got into you today?"

Davies shrugged, clearly not feeling well. "I guess it's just all this terrorism business, Bob. Gives me the ol' heebie-jeebies."

"It's not like you, Roger. Why don't you go down and wait in my limousine. I'll just be a moment."

"I think I'll do that. The air-conditioning will perk me up."

The older man began walking quickly down the bridge as the governor crossed to the waiting reporters. On the southern shore, the first of the cars moved past the state troopers and began the drive across the three-mile span.

BISHOP HIT THE GAS and the old Chevy's engine took hold. He swerved out of traffic and cut in two cars ahead. The driver behind him hit his horn. Bishop continued to accelerate, his eyes glued to the silver

Lincoln as it pulled into traffic. He reached the rest-stop exit ramp two cars behind it.

Traffic coming off the old span onto the two-lane approach forced him into line. He drove, looking ahead for an opening and saw it when the state troopers waved the traffic onto the new bridge. There was no oncoming traffic and wouldn't be until cars began arriving from the other side of Tampa Bay.

He floored it, pulled out and drove until he paralleled the silver Lincoln. Drivers honked, and almost immediately the shrill siren of a police car cut the air. The bearded terrorist at the wheel of the Lincoln looked at the Chevy pulling up beside him. His mouth dropped open. He accelerated, the luxury car's powerful engine quickly outpacing the older Chevy up the gradual incline of the bridge.

What the Chevy lacked in pickup, it made up for in speed. As the two cars approached the crest of the bridge, Bishop pulled ahead, ramming the Lincoln from the side. People at the top of the bridge ran for the sides while policemen and guards around the governor drew their weapons. Press photographers jockeyed for position and aimed their cameras at the speeding cars.

The Lincoln skidded, scraping the concrete railings and leaving a hail of sparks. The driver recovered, and the car sped ahead of the Chevy again. Keeping one hand on the wheel, the terrorist fumbled with the briefcase on the seat beside him, undoing the clasps. Then he threw it into the back seat.

Bishop saw it. He had one minute left.

Slowly the old Chevy pulled ahead of the Lincoln as the two cars reached the top of the Skyway's arch.

Bishop heard gunfire, and felt bullets hit the car. The sheriff's men were shooting for the tires, still interested in stopping, not killing. He knew that would change momentarily.

He pulled ahead of the Lincoln and jerked the steering wheel hard to the right, cutting in front of the terrorist's car. The Lincoln smashed into him sideways, wrecking the Chevy and smashing it sixty feet down the bridge before it slammed against a concrete abutment. The steel suspension cables quivered with the shock of the collision. The Lincoln spun sideways, smashing over the concrete guardrail, and coming to a stop with its front wheels over the edge of the bridge. The tires spun, and the radiator blew a cloud of steam over Tampa Bay, eighty feet below.

Bishop leaped from the car and ran toward the Lincoln amid shouts from the police and the sound of bullets whining over his head. A group of photographers had climbed a guardrail and aimed their cameras at the scoop of a lifetime. The merc dived for the Lincoln, jerking open the driver's door.

Bullets slammed into the car as the surprised terrorist backed away on the seat with his feet in front of him, kicking Bishop's face fanatically. The Canadian ignored the blows and crawled inside and reached for the briefcase on the back seat.

The terrorist threw himself across Bishop's arm, his hands like claws closing over the merc's eyes.

There was no time left, but there was still one way out. The only way.

Straightening his leg, Bishop jabbed at the floor under the steering wheel until his foot connected with the accelerator. The engine roared, and the Lincoln surged forward over the side of the Skyway, plunging toward the cool blue waters of Tampa Bay.

"WAIT! GO BACK!" Walker Jessup shouted to the chopper pilot when he saw the two cars racing up the span of the newly completed bridge.

By the time the helicopter had returned to hover off the side of the Skyway, the old car had collided with the Lincoln almost knocking it off the bridge. The Fixer raised the field glasses to his eyes, as a barefooted man jumped from the older car.

"Oh my God!" He kept the binoculars pressed to his eyes with one hand and reached for the radio transmitter. "It's Walker Jessup reporting. Get those men on the bridge to stop shooting! Stop them shooting! That's one of my boys down there! The Lincoln is terrorist. It's got to be! Yes, stop them!"

He dropped the transmitter. He was screaming into it. It made no sense to the operator, and there was no way the operator could stop the state troopers in time.

"Get down there!" he yelled at the pilot. The air force man looked at him as if he was crazy. The chopper dropped on top of the Skyway, and the pilot moved it into a hover beside the central span.

Bishop ran through a hail of bullets and leaped inside the Lincoln.

Jessup threw aside his seat belt and moved his bulky weight to the cabin. He slid the side door back and, gripping a safety handle, leaned out of the chopper, shouting to the state troopers.

"Stop! Stop them! Someone stop them!"

Suddenly the back tires of the Lincoln spun madly, and clouds of stinking smoke rose from under the car as it pushed forward across the guard rail.

"No!" Jessup shouted until his throat was scraped raw. The big Lincoln plunged toward the water far below.

Halfway down, it blew. Debris rained in the water. White smoke and flame lingered briefly in midair. Ocean winds caught the smoke, dissipating it into a gray cloud that obscured the dignitaries, the police, the photographers, the chopper, the dead and the silence that fell over the great arching span of the Skyway Bridge.

14

The TV news reporter stood in front of a gray stone building. Snowflakes swirled in the air around him. He spoke intensely into a microphone, occasionally arching his back to make a point.

"Even though positive identification of the terrorist on the Skyway Bridge was made by Janet Rush, his former wife, the RCMP, coordinating their actions with the FBI, have released few details about the life of Geoff Bishop. A decorated Canadian Armed Forces pilot, he later became a commercial jetliner pilot, one of the highest paid in the industry. For a time, he was even famous when, because of faulty instrument readings, the airplane he was flying ran out of gas over the Canadian prairies. He was able to save the lives of hundreds of passengers by bringing the airplane down on a stretch of the Trans Canada Highway.

"According to Mrs. Rush, Bishop left the airline he worked for, disgruntled, convinced the company had given him a raw deal. Although Mrs. Rush says she continued to receive her alimony checks regularly, she rarely saw him. To quote the terrorist's ex-wife, 'He would disappear for weeks, sometimes months at a time, and refuse to say where he was going. He never told me what line of work he was in, but he always seemed to have lots of money.'

"Where did Geoff Bishop go wrong? At what point did he take the shadowy path that led him into the evil world of terrorism? How did he become involved in the bizarre plot to attack Florida at the height of the tourist season? Why did he attack a respected international technology salesman, dragging him over the bridge to his death? Law enforcement agencies around the world are seeking clues to answer these questions, but dead men tell no tales. We may never know. Next, Dick Rainer in Tampa speaks to the elderly couple Bishop terrorized just before the attempt on the Sunshine Skyway. From Montreal this is Jay Chio..."

"Shut up! Shut up!" Alex Nanos pushed the power button on the TV remote and raised his good arm to throw the remote at the television screen. His other arm and shoulder were immobilized under layers of white bandages.

"Cool it, Alex." Lee Hatton grabbed the remote just as it left the Greek's hand. Nanos sank weakly into the pillows of his hospital bed. "You're barely off the critical list. Just take it easy. You're damn lucky to be alive."

"Christ, Lee. Make them stop. Claude, Billy Two, can't anyone make them stop it?"

"They're working on it, man," Claude Hayes said, clamping a big hand firmly on Nanos's shoulder. He stood on the other side of the hospital bed. "Jessup and the colonel. You know if there's anything anyone can do, they'll do it."

"Look at this shit," Nanos said, lifting a copy of the *St. Petersburg Times* from the bed, then dropping it with disgust. Beneath the screaming headlines was a picture taken by one of the photographers on the Skyway Bridge on Florida's day of reckoning. Geoff Bishop was haggard but clearly recognizable as he jumped from the old Chevy and ran toward the Lincoln.

Nanos looked up at the team's medical expert, the merc who was closest to the missing man. "Lee, how can you take it?"

Hatton's face tightened as Claude Hayes and Billy Two fell silent. They had kept their eyes on her in the two days since the mission had ended. Like the rest of them, she showed anger rather than sorrow. Sorrow, they knew, was her private business, like the private affair she and Bishop had once had. It was territory that none of them dared to trespass upon even now. In her private moments, Lee would let the tears come. Later. Grief was a luxury for any professional soldier, regardless of sex.

Nate Beck entered and, sensing the delicate moment, remained silent. More newspapers were folded under his arms.

Lee moved from the bed toward the window and spoke softly.

"We all knew the risks, and we accepted them as the price we had to pay to do this kind of work."

"Yeah, but none of us ever thought it would turn into this," said Claude Hayes. "The real terrorist turns out to be a respected international technology salesman for a major U.S. defence department contractor. His cover holds. Both men are killed. Our guy takes the rap as public enemy number one. It's unbelievable.''

Beck removed his jacket and laid it across a chair. "It's amazing, isn't it, how the secrecy of our job gives all of us typical terrorist profiles. Like Geoff's mysterious absences and unknown but substantial sources of income."

"None of us ever thought it would be used against us," said Hayes. "Not this way."

"You ain't seen nothing yet. That wasn't the only photograph that was taken."

Beck opened the newspaper under his arm and threw it onto Nanos's bed. It was the *World Weekly News*. Under the usual teasers about a new miracle diet plan and a thirteen-year-old boy marrying an eighty-seven-year-old woman, the main headline screamed, Giant Aliens From Outer Space Save Florida! Underneath, a very blurry photograph showed Liam O'Toole hanging on to the balcony of the Daytona Beach Hotel, swinging the young student on his back to safety.

"What in hell," Hayes muttered, picking the tabloid up and flipping to the story on page three. "At least someone got it right."

"Well, the press isn't the only one who's confused," Nanos said, forcing a little smile in Billy Two's direction. "Look at the bandage around that loony injun's arm. Hawk Spirit promised invulnerability as usual, but from what I hear, he got a little mixed up between the Osage and the giant teddy bear."

"Lies are like spiders," Billy Two said gruffly, employing one of his metaphors. "They spin their own webs of deceit. Hawk Spirit tests me. I have made peace with him again."

"I could use a coffee," Claude Hayes suggested boisterously. "Anyone else?"

Nate and Billy Two took Hayes up on the offer, and the mercs headed for the hospital cafeteria, leaving Lee Hatton alone with Alex Nanos.

"Is that part of the job?" Lee asked softly, still looking out the window at downtown St. Petersburg. "To live a lie? To be tested?"

"Not like this, Lee," Nanos said. He stared at the blank ceiling, his thoughts moving among the confusion of the last days.

Lee moved to the bed and sat beside the Greek. She spoke with her head down, reluctantly and with reticence. "You...you don't remember anything more today, do you?"

Alex Nanos reached for her hand and squeezed it. He bit his lip and shook his head sadly.

"I've tried, Lee. God knows I've tried. One moment we were watching the yacht. Next thing I knew, well, it's a blur. I think we were on the yacht at one point, unbelievable as that seems. I'm sure we were on another boat. I remember Geoff putting his finger to his lips, warning me to be silent. Then I remember on the beach, when he left me.... That's all. I ..."

The Greek's voice broke, and his eyes clouded with tears. He swallowed and breathed heavily, fighting against his own emotions. He faked a quiet laugh.

"Guess the medication screws me up." He was silent a moment, thoughtful. When he spoke again, it was with great difficulty. "Lee, it's awful. I just keep thinking of what I should have done. I feel responsible, somehow...like ..."

Lee clutched his hand as the Greek's voice broke again. "You're not, Alex. You're not. Don't say that. Ever."

Alex could speak no more. When he looked at Hatton, a tear left her eye and traveled slowly down her cheek. She made no attempt to brush it away.

They sat in silence.

"Where's the colonel today?" Nanos asked finally.

"He took off in the chopper. Said he had to see a man about a dog."

Nanos looked at her, puzzled.

The woman mercenary shrugged. "I'm not sure, but I think I know what it means."

Alex Nanos nodded. "It means he's working on it."

THE GOVERNOR OF FLORIDA leaned back in his padded leather chair, and looked out the windows of his Tallahassee office.

How does spring come to Florida? he thought. Gradually. First, the azaleas bloom—great bushes of glowing purple everywhere. Then the oleanders as the temperatures creep into the eighties, and trees show little traces of new greenery among the leaves. Birds become suddenly busy, building nests under the eaves of houses, and the fat silver mullet leap athletically above the surface of brackish ponds. The tourists leave, and Florida settles back into its casual Southern pace with its take-it-easy attitude.

Today, though, it was pouring rain. The driving tropical storm had been lashing the state for two days. It was unusual at this time of year, and for a Floridian, more than one gray-and-gloomy day in a row was almost unheard of. The governor reflected that nature was in sympathy with man, with the tragedy that had overcome his beloved state.

Nile Barrabas had saved them from an even worse slaughter. His team of trained mercenaries had eliminated the threat—for the time being. But innocence was gone from America's winter playground, probably forever. Florida had been deflowered, a virgin raped.

The buzz of his intercom was followed by his secretary's voice. "Mr. Walker Jessup has arrived for his appointment, sir."

"Send him in. Oh, by the way, have you reached Roger Davies yet?"

"No, sir, the servant at his house informed me that he had gone hunting but was unable to say where. I'm still trying to reach someone at his office who knows."

"Stay on it. I want to see him as soon as possible."

The overweight Texan lumbered through the door of the executive office. The two men shook hands, and the governor motioned him to a chair. "My campaign manager cum political mentor has absented himself for the last two days," the politician explained as the Fixer lowered his bulk into a chair. "We have to discuss the effect of the recent terrorist actions on the campaign for the Senate.''

"Looks like you're coming out ahead because of your handling of the crisis, and despite the casualties.''

"It still requires some delicate manoeuvering, though, Walker. Now, what can I do for you?''

"Bishop.''

The governor sighed and swiveled his chair sideways so he could see out the window again.

"And that isn't the only thing,'' the Fixer continued. "The yacht that was found scuttled, the one Barrabas's two men had under surveillance—it was registered to Gorgon Incorporated. Same company that built the submersibles. Same company that the terrorist working under the cover of a technology salesman had dealings with. So when does that investigation start?''

"What investigation, Walker? Gorgon Incorporated reported that the yacht was stolen from the Jacksonville marina a week ago. And may I remind you, no evidence has surfaced to confirm that the technology salesman had any terrorist connections.''

"They reported it stolen yesterday!'' Jessup roared with anger. "With some lame excuse about waiting a week for an internal investigation to be completed!''

The governor winced. "You've been involved in these things before, Walker. Gorgon is a major defence contractor, very powerful, very well connected. You can't just march in and demand an investigation. I'm doing what I can.''

Jessup nodded skeptically. "Yep," he drawled, lapsing into his native Texan accent. "I bin round long enough to know when someone's tiptoeing on the slope of a volcano trying not to git his ass burned. And Bishop? What are you going to do to clear his name? You know as well as I do who the real terrorist on the bridge was."

The governor stood, turning his back on the Fixer. He walked to the tall casement windows overlooking the gardens of Tallahassee's silver-domed capital building and stood with his hands behind his back.

"Nothing."

Jessup rose, anger flooding through him. "What in hell you mean, 'nothing'?"

The governor spun around. "Your boys knew the risks and accepted them."

"They knew the risk that they might die. They accepted the fact that what they did they did without acknowledgment, recognition or any reward other than a cash payment. But not this, Mr. Governor. Not this. Not one of them being turned into a villain by some chain of accident and circumstance, his name besmirched in death. That wasn't part of the deal."

"But that's the way it turned out. Don't you see that!" This time the governor was yelling, the conflict evident in his craggy face. He walked to his desk and leaned across at Jessup.

"Don't you see?" the governor said, still shouting. "What the Soldiers of Barrabas did here in Florida was illegal. It was illegal, Jessup. We knew it and so did they. That was the deal. Any attempt I make to clear Bishop's name will expose this covert action team to the scrutiny of the press and any politician who wants to make an issue out of it." His voice dropped. "Then what'll happen, Walker? What'll happen next time?"

Jessup breathed silently. He knew what the governor's answer would be before he'd made the appointment. And although every emotion and every ounce of his being fought against it, the part of him that they called the Fixer knew the governor was right.

"I sympathize, Walker. Really I do. But you know as well as I do that clearing Geoff Bishop's name will destroy your team."

The governor moved out from behind the desk and walked to Jessup's side, clapping an arm around his broad shoulders.

"We've all been through a hell of a lot. A band of ruthless men was loosed upon this fair state and blood has flown as a result. Without your men it would have been far worse, and as the duly elected representative of the people, they have my gratitude and admiration. Florida owes them much, and Florida can never be the same again."

The Texan pulled away from the politician. His face was a tight white mask, concealing his torment. He felt low. He felt that he had personally betrayed Nile Barrabas and the SOBs. He hoped like hell those brave soldiers wouldn't feel that way. But, if they did, he couldn't blame them.

"Why did they choose us?" the governor sighed as Jessup reached the door. "Why did terrorism come to paradise?"

Walker Jessup turned as he reached the door. "Paradise, Governor? Florida's not paradise. That's an illusion that you and everyone else here has created, like Dracula's castle and Dream Land and all the other tacky things in this giant toy town. It's nice to believe in, great for entertainment, but it ain't true."

The two men looked at each other for a moment, both of them at a loss for words.

"Welcome to reality," Jessup said with finality. He left, closing the door firmly behind him.

THE DRIVING TROPICAL RAIN STORM rocked the helicopter as it approached the Florida coast from the Everglades.

"Colonel Barrabas," Landry Carter, shouted over the noise of the engine and the storm, "that camp down there will be a field of mud. If we land, it's liable to suck the skids in, and we won't get out until the sun dries it enough for us to dig out."

"How long can you hover?" Barrabas asked.

"As long as we have gas," the pilot said.

The mercenary leader nodded. "Then hover. What I have to do won't take me long."

The secret Everglades camp, half a mile to the west where the river of grass met the ocean, was still invisible in the driving rain. Barrabas pushed himself up from his cockpit seat and slipped into the cabin, where Liam O'Toole handed him a MAC-10 submachine gun.

"Loaded. You want spare mags?"

"Are you sure he's alone down there?" Barrabas asked.

The Irish merc nodded. "Even the chauffeur of the governor's best friend liked the look and feel of five crisp hundred-dollar bills. 'Course they were wrapped inside my fist when he finally told me. Seems Mr. Davies makes a habit of coming out here for some illegal alligator hunting whenever the camp's not being used by law enforcement authorities or game wardens. Sure you don't want me down there with you, Colonel?"

Barrabas shook his head. "This is one on one, Liam. But keep your eyes peeled in case he does have friends."

A few minutes later the chopper descended slowly toward the camp, and Barrabas leaped from the cabin. Carter had been right; Barrabas landed in a field of mud, and his boots sank up to his ankles.

The chopper backed off. Barrabas pulled up the collar of his fatigue jacket as egg-sized rain drops spattered against him, soaking him to the skin in seconds. The mud slurped in protest as he strained to yank his feet up and move forward.

The camp appeared to be deserted. A large cabin cruiser, the cockpit and bridge covered with protective drop cloths, was tied to the pier. Barrabas looked about and made his way across to the cabin that the governor had used for the conference several days earlier.

Near the front door, the three alligators glared at him, resentment glowing in their yellow reptilian eyes. As he stepped past them, they scurried away from him in the mud, straining against the stout ropes around their necks that bound them to the wooden stakes. From a distance of ten feet, they glared at him again warily, snapping their mouths open and shut to reveal their rows of tiny sharp teeth. They were hungry. They hadn't been fed since the rain started.

Like Barrabas, the alligators knew a secret: that the human animal was the most terrible of them all. The gators had learned it at the hands of one who was particularly evil. Roger Davies. The man had left his signature beside one of the buildings. A half dozen dead gators lay stacked like cord wood. He was here.

Barrabas pulled a razor-sharp Bowie knife from the sheath under his jacket and bent to sever the ropes that bound the captive alligators. An aggressive one snapped at him. He threw it the end of the rope. Unsure of their new freedom, the three reptiles backed slowly away. The big snapper turned and headed for the nearby water.

Suddenly Barrabas heard the roar of an engine. He swung around as a Land Rover with oversized tires slammed through the mud straight at him. He jumped to the side, cutting past the front fender, rolling in the muck. He heard gun shots and felt the wet ground splatter beside his head.

Quickly he was up, swinging his MAC-10 around and loosing half the mag across the side of the Land Rover. He followed up with a leap onto the vehicle. Roger Davies rose from the driver's seat, swinging his double-barreled shotgun to keep Barrabas away.

The mercenary ducked. He slammed the back of the MAC-10 into Davies's gut, throwing him off balance. Still in gear, the all-terrain vehicle moved forward. Davies teetered and fell backward with a short wail of surprise, disappearing beneath the wheels of the Land Rover.

A shriek cut through the pounding rain. Barrabas dropped into the driver's seat and stopped the vehicle. He hopped out and ran back.

Roger Davies lay on his butt in the mud, writhing in pain. His legs had been crushed. The jagged splintered end of a broken bone protruded from the leg of his pants. He whimpered, pushing himself away from Barrabas with his hands. Rain splattered against his muddy face. The three alligators watched from the bank, studying the man's dilemma with cold reptilian intelligence.

"How's it feel, Davies?" Barrabas stood over him, holding the submachine gun loosely at his side. He had no more use for it. "Like all those people slaughtered at Wonderworld or burned alive at Daytona Beach or in the trailer park. Or like Geoff Bishop, blown to pieces so small that the sharks probably didn't even get much to eat. How's it feel? Tell me, Davies, because I've always wanted know how it feels when a guy like you tastes his own blood."

"How...how'd you know?" Davies gasped, his head rolling with the waves of pain from his legs.

"Like we used to say in military intelligence, I walked the cat back. Gorgon Incorporated, or someone in it, built the submersibles and arranged for the diversion of the NATO shipment to terrorists. Gorgon used the corporate yacht for some purpose we haven't quite figured out and supplied cover for the terrorist who was going to blow up the Skyway. Wasn't it interesting to find out you were on the board of directors and a major shareholder. But that wasn't the clincher.'' He paused, looking at the traitor squirming in the mud.

''Wh-what?''

''I knew the terrorists had an inside source of information. After my men's surveillance of the yacht was blown, I knew it had to be someone at the meeting with the governor here. Stupid. No, not stupid. Just that you and whoever you were working with were so confident of success, so arrogant in your bloodthirsty scheming, in all the power and privilege that's gone to your head that you didn't even try to take precautions. I had my computer man check telephone-radio transmissions. You were the only person to send messages from this camp after the meeting. It had to be you.''

Roger Davies began shaking uncontrollably. Barrabas knelt and looked him square in the face.

''What I want to know is who you were working with. And why.''

''Never,'' Davies said, spitting the word out angrily, gasping again for air. ''Our work is too important. You won't defeat us.''

The traitor's eyes drifted sideways, and he held his breath. Barrabas looked.

Scenting blood, the three carnivorous reptiles had come closer. Their yellow eyes stared balefully at the two men. The gators were meat eaters, experts at the game of predation, singling out the weakest and most vulnerable prey, separating it from the herd and attacking. They weren't looking at Barrabas. They were looking at Davies. But something else shone in their eyes that Barrabas recognized. Hatred.

The mercenary commando stood, towering over Davies. "That's what I thought you'd say."

Davies reached a tentative arm toward the grim-faced colonel. He opened his mouth to say something but stopped, seeing the refusal already in Barrabas's eyes.

"And even if you did tell, you'd only implicate other powerful people. People I couldn't get to. What you and your ilk always forget is that there is justice in the universe, Davies. Sometimes it's a helluva lot more cruel than human justice. But it exists."

Barrabas wiped the rain and muck from his face. The chopper was hovering at the other side of the camp. He turned and started walking toward it.

"Wait!" Davies called. "God, no! Wait!"

Barrabas glanced over his shoulder. The alligators had taken their cue from his departure. They crawled on their bellies toward the old crippled man in the mud.

Davies fell forward, desperate, using his arms to pull himself a few precious feet after the colonel. Casually, the yellow-eyed reptiles approached.

"Nooo! Pleeease! I'll tell you everything! Everything! I'll name names!"

What was the point, thought Barrabas. Name names and the names will belong to people who had put themselves beyond the reach of human justice. But he could wait until they made their move again. And they would move again—of that he was certain. Then he would smash them. Roger Davies, the traitor, screamed until his voice grew weaker. Barrabas waved to the chopper. It moved slowly across the sea of mud toward him, the wind stream from the rotor whipping the tropical storm into a frenzy.

He bent his head against the hard rain and remained that way until the screams ended. Geoff Bishop, a good man gone. Now he was avenged.

The helicopter door slid open in front of him and Barrabas reached for it. His job was done, paid off in anger and more sorrow.

There was no point in crying. Tears made no statement in the driving rain.

ERIC HELM

VIETNAM: GROUND ZERO

An elite jungle fighting group of strike-and-hide specialists fight a dirty war half a world away from home. This is more than action adventure. Every novel in this series is a piece of Vietnam history brought to life, from the Battle for Hill 875 to the Tet Offensive and the terror of the infamous Hanoi Hilton POW camp, told through the eyes of an American Special Forces squad. These books cut close to the bone, telling it the way it really was.

"Vietnam at Ground Zero is where this book is written. The author has been there, and he knows. I salute him and I recommend this book to my friends."

—Don Pendleton,
creator of The Executioner

Now available from Gold Eagle Books, #1 publisher of adventures.

VGZ-1-R